Lust And Bl...
By Mel Pa...

Copyright page

© Copyright 2024 by Melissia Pate

All rights reserved.

The contents of this book, "Lust And Blood," are protected by United States copyright laws. The content may not be duplicated, transmitted, quoted, paraphrased, or reproduced, in whole or in part, without the written permission of the author.

The contents of this book are fictional. Any of the characters or their names used in this book, locations, described, or incidents are not intended to refer to any place, or actual event, and any resemblance is coincidental.

authormelpate@gmail.com

Chapter 1

Sam

Today has been fairly quiet, I think as I finish the last of the invoices, placing them in the to be filed tray. I lean back in my chair, staring out at the bustling street. The sun is low in the sky, and its warm hues feel amazing on my face. I close my eyes, enjoying it and let my mind wonder.

Every day feels the same. I get up, work, then go home, ordering takeout. Will it always be this way? Each day blurring into the next?

The rhythmic hum of cars outside is relaxing. It's probably why I sleep so well at night, except for the nights... No, I won't think about them. I sigh, opening my eyes, spotting the stack of mail. Right on top, I see another letter from that damn developer company. They are persistent. I grab the letter opener and open it. Why do I even bother? We always say no and they just keep sending them. Each one grows more insistent. Don't they understand everything isn't about money?

Uncle Fred and Roger opened this place in their 20s after getting out of the military. Gearhead Custom's is a staple on the Southside of the city. It's been here longer than I've been alive. My eyebrows furrowed and frustration built as I read the letter. We've all put our heart and soul into this place. We thrive on taking antique muscle cars and breathing new life into them. These idiots think we'll sell the property so they can build a high-rise or put condos here. They've lost their minds.

Suddenly, I hear raised voices in the reception area and I jump out of my chair, taking purposeful steps to see what the hell's happening. When I throw my office door open, I see a red-faced man pointing at sweet Jules, our receptionist yelling. "You've had it for 3 weeks, and I want it now!"

Oh, hell no, he isn't. I rush forward, firmly planting my feet and squaring my shoulders, standing between them. Making sure Jules is safely behind me. "What seems to be the problem?"

The man straightens and eyes me carefully before speaking. "My Plymouth Superbird has been here three weeks and still isn't finished. I want it now!" I cock a brow at him. He's in his twenties, wearing a suit that's at least worth a grand, a Rolex on his wrist, and shoes that could pay several months' rent for most people. So the arrogant rich boy bought himself a muscle car, brought it here for us to customize and thinks it happens with a snap of a finger.

I shake my head at him and speak to Jules, never taking my eyes off of him. "Do you have the quote we provided Mr..." I pause, waiting for this prick's name.

He curls his lip up but gives it. "Stein," he says, like I was supposed to know it already.

I nod and hold my hand out, waiting for Jules to give it to me. She is an amazing bubbly person who does a great job running the counter. For some dipshit to treat her this way pisses me off. "Here," Jules says, placing it in my hand. I briefly glance over the information down to his signature at the bottom before returning my gaze to his.

I lock eyes with Mr. More Money than brains and grin. "Well, Mr. Stein, do you remember us giving you a written quote stating it would take 3 months for us to complete the rebuild and paint, the amount of the job, you signing it, and us giving you a carbon copy?" I cock my head to the side, enjoying the fact I just called him out.

I see him clenching his fists at his side, and Jules steps back. Good, because this man doesn't look smart or stable. He does, however, look and sound entitled, but I'm about to school him. Mr. Stein raises his bony finger, pointing at my hand holding the quote. "I don't care what that says. I want my car now. So how much is it going to cost?" I burst out laughing. So he thinks he can throw a black card down, and his car will magically be ready?

He reached into the breast pocket of his jacket, pulling a wallet out, and I held up my hand. "Mr. Stein, money doesn't just make things happen. The job takes three months."

He snarls, stepping close, "Then produce my car, and I'll take it elsewhere."

LUST AND BLOOD

With a hard look, I meet his stare. "Fine. Pay for what's been done so far, and you're free to take it wherever you like."

"You bitch, you've disrespected me and you didn't complete the job. I'm not paying a dime now!"

So, being me, I laugh again just to annoy him. "No payment, no car."

His face twists in rage before lunging forward, going for my throat. Instinct took over, and I reacted. Using a maneuver Uncle Fred taught me, grabbing his hand with mine, I bend his thumb backward and twist my body behind him, taking his arm. His thumb snaps, breaking, and I now have his arm pinned between his shoulder blades. Mr. Stein squeals like a banshee on crack at the pain radiating through his shoulder. I stomp the back of his leg, forcing him to drop into a kneeling position. "Now, Mr. Stein, attacking a woman isn't acceptable. Attacking me is stupid. You're going to apologize. Then I'm going to release you so you can stand. Once you do, you will leave and not come back until you have transportation to remove your vehicle from the premises and pay the bill in full for services rendered to date. Are we clear?"

He nods frantically, trying to breathe through the pain. I pull his arm slightly higher and he apologizes. I grin, looking at Jules, who has her hands covering her mouth in shock, and her eyes are as wide as saucers.

Releasing him, I step back and to the side, keeping myself positioned between him and Jules. "Transportation will be here tomorrow morning when you open check in hand."

I cock my head to the side, observing him. I don't trust him as far as I can throw him. "Cash." One word and I see a flash of something behind his eyes, but he nods and storms out. I watch him leave until Jules jumps on me from behind, wrapping her arms around me, squealing. *That was so badass, Sam.* I laugh at her antics, turn, making her release me.

I shrug and smile. "Just doing my part to put pricks in their place."

I chuckle, letting the tension leave me, then I look into the corner, glad we have security cameras. The brat might call the cops. Then I remember the events and know it wouldn't do any good. He attacked me first. They would probably just laugh that a woman handed him his ass.

Sam picks the quote off the floor I dropped earlier and sighs. "You need to let Uncle Fred and Roger know."

I nod and walk towards the back bays, knowing they aren't going to like this. When I enter, I see them hoisting a rebuilt engine back into a beautiful Mustang. It's a nice-looking car, but not as nice as mine. Once they step away, I approach and tell them everything.

Roger, my Uncle Fred's army buddy, crosses his arms over his chest and grunts. "Why didn't you yell at us to handle it?"

I smile at how overprotective he is. He helped Uncle Fred raise me and would have definitely squashed the bug. "Because I could handle him. Skinny trust fund brat with more mouth than muscle." I shrug and smile. He nods, and I look at Uncle Fred, who is opening a bottle of water.

He takes a long drink, then screws the cap back on. "It's in bay 4. We'll lock things down tight tonight. He can have the thing. We're backed up as it is and don't need the work, anyway." I nod and grin, feeling relieved. Uncle Fred is amazing, but I hate the thought of disappointing him. I work hard every day to build the business up so he doesn't have to worry. We rarely lose a customer, but when it happens, my stomach is always in knots.

He eyes me carefully, and his lip quirks up. "You did good, Sam. Sometimes we need to let our crazy out."

I roll my eyes and laugh. He has called me that since I was 16 and did something really stupid. "I'm not crazy, just impulsive," I say with a huff and walk away.

Walking past the breakroom to my office, I see Jules sitting at the table playing with a pack of crackers, looking lost. Concern stops me in my tracks and I enter, sitting across from her. She raises her head, looking at me with a smile, but it's forced. This isn't my way too cheerful friend that I normally want to give a chill pill. "What's wrong?" She can't fool me, and she knows it.

Jules plays with the crackers and doesn't meet my eyes. "You know, Steve and I have gone out a few times." I nod when she looks at me, guessing where this is going. Steve is another douchebag with money and thinks he's a bad boy. I see him for what he is, a player. But Jules doesn't see that. She's always attracted to the bad boy type. The wrong type of bad boy. I squeeze her hand, waiting for her to continue.

She clears her throat, looking nervous. "He's been pushing, and I'm not ready yet."

LUST AND BLOOD

I dig my nails into my thigh with my free hand and grit my teeth. So the prick wants to get laid like I thought. Jules is beautiful and sweet. Way too good for a player. "Look, Jules, don't let anyone push you into something you're not ready for. When the time's right or the right person comes along, you'll know it."

Jules grins and comes over, hugging me tight. "Thanks for always listening."

I squeeze her back before stepping away. "Always, let's close up shop." It has to be after 6 p.m. We walk through, shut the lights off, flip the sign on the door, and lock it. After saying goodnight to everyone, they leave and I go upstairs to my little apartment. I moved out of Uncle Fred's house when I was 18, thinking I was cramping his style. The man rarely dates. Turns out it's a choice after having his heart broken by some woman who couldn't wait until his term was up in the military. I guess he doesn't want to go down heartbreak road again.

Once I enter the apartment, I kick my boots off, make my way to the couch, plop down, and pull out my cell phone. What do I want to eat tonight? Pizza! I hit speed dial for the local pizza joint and grab a cold beer, waiting.

I hear a vehicle outside with the music up so loud the base is rattling my windows. Going to the exterior door, I look out the peephole. It's Steve in his little red Porsche. The passenger window lowers, and he stares at the building, then shakes his head, rolling the window up. I guess he can't tell time. We closed 15 minutes ago; he missed Jules. With a sigh, I watch him peel out of the parking lot. I wish she would dump his ass and wait for someone who would treat her right. I grit my teeth, thinking about the last time he was in the garage to pick her up. He spoke to her like she was beneath him. I'd love to kick his balls up, introducing them to his tonsils.

Chapter 2

Jules

The sun is setting as I arrive home. Grabbing my things, I exit the car with a sigh, thinking what a long day it's been. I remove my tennis shoes and go to the kitchen to get a glass of water. It's so quiet, I think, looking out the window over the sink. With Mom and Dad retired and living in Florida, the evenings get lonely, and Sam never wants to go out.

Looking across the yard, I see Uncle Fred's house next door, and a flood of childhood memories washes over me. Sam and I grew up as neighbors and have been best friends for as long as I can remember. I smile, thinking about today. Sam, crazy as ever, kicked that man's ass. I can't help but giggle. A part of me wishes I was as brave and quick-thinking as she is. Sam's always been fierce and independent. Qualities I admire.

With a shake of my head, I open the cabinet, removing a can of soup for dinner. Hmm, maybe a good movie tonight. The sound of a car pulling into the driveway catches my attention, and I peek out the window.

Steve's sleek red Porche is pulling in and the booming music is echoing through our quiet neighborhood. Steve is a wealthy bad boy type and is gorgeous. I couldn't ignore his charm and compliments forever. We've been out a few times. Despite my better judgment, I'm drawn to him. Me and my stupid hormones love his type.

When three loud knocks come from the door, I walk into the living room, opening it with a smile. But it fades when I see his expression. He looks agitated, and his jaw's clenched. Steve steps through the door, grabs me, and crashes his lips on mine. I'm out of breath when he pulls back, and a little stunned. "Why weren't you at the shop when I arrived?"

His voice is sharp, and I'm taken aback. "We close at 6 p.m., you know that," I say, wondering what his problem is.

Steve reaches up, gripping the back of my hair, tilting my face further back. His fingers are digging into my scalp, and I suck in a quick breath. "Watch your tone with me," he says, then his expression softens, looking me up and down. "Get changed, baby; We're going to dinner."

I'm torn between confusion and frustration until he caresses my face and gives me that brilliant white smile.

I guess a meal out would be nice. With a resigned smile, I nod and go into my room, changing into a simple knee-length black dress and heels.

The ride to the restaurant is quiet, but he holds my hand, rubbing circles on the back. Why am I always attracted to the bad boys? I wonder as I stare out the window. Once we're seated and order things change from quiet to uncomfortable.

Steve dominates the conversation, discussing his achievements at his father's advertising firm. My only interaction is a smile when he compliments me. The things he says to me make me feel beautiful, and he's attractive, but everything else about him makes me uneasy. There's a voice screaming in my head, telling me to stay away from him.

On the drive home, he takes my hand and begins tracing slow circles on my wrist, sending a shiver up my spine. My mind says one thing, but my body reacts instantly to his touch.

When we arrive back at my house, his demeanor seems to change. I unlock the door, thinking he will kiss me goodnight and return to his car, but he doesn't. As soon as the door's unlocked, he pushes it open and pulls us both inside by wrapping his arm around my waist.

Steve swings me around so my back is against the wall, and his body presses into mine. He immediately begins kissing me roughly, and his hand grabs my breast, squeezing. This isn't sweet. It's demanding and forceful, scaring me a little.

I plant both hands on his chest and shove him off with all my might. My heart is racing, and both fear and anger have me shaking. "Stop!"

Steve laughs and shakes his head. "You fucking tease." I'm stunned by his words; his hand connects with my face before I know what's happening. Pain shoots through my mouth in its wake, leaving a throbbing sting behind. He really just slapped me? He hit me?

LUST AND BLOOD

Tears fill my eyes as I look up at him. "Get out!" My demanding scream has left my throat feeling raw. Emotions flood me, and I push him backward towards the door.

His face turns soft again, but I see past it. It's not real; it's a mask he wears to get his way. Why did I not see that before?

I jerk the door open, and he looks disappointed. "I'm sorry, Jules. Let's forget this and have a nice evening together."

Is he serious? "It's way too late for that. Get out." I lock it behind him as soon as he's past the door. My hands shake, and I feel foolish. I reach up, touching my throbbing mouth, and see blood on my trembling hand.

Knowing I don't want to be alone, I fish my phone out of my purse and dial Sam. As soon as she picks up, I cry like an idiot. "What's wrong?" I can hear the worry in her voice.

With a sniffle, I gather myself. "Something happened with Steve. Can you come over?" I hear shuffling and keys rattling.

"I'm on my way. Did he touch you?" Sam's voice is low and deadly, making me reach up and touch my lip. I refuse to lie to her, though. Besides, she'll see my face.

"Yes," I say, entering the bedroom to change out of this dress.

I hear a door open and shut before she speaks. "I'm on my way. Lock the door." The line goes dead, and I sigh. Shit, I need a friend right now, but I may have to calm her down.

After changing, I wet a washcloth in the bathroom and looked into the mirror. My face looks horrible. My blonde hair is a mess, my mascara's streaked, and I have blood on my mouth and chin. I cringe when I see my lip in the mirror. It's split and already swelling. "Asshole," I say, then hiss at the pain.

I do my best to clean my face up before Sam gets here. True to her word, I hear her Camaro roaring into the driveway fifteen minutes after we hung up. Bursting through the living room door with a key, she has a concerned expression etched on her face.

One look at me, and her face is red with anger, but she engulfs me in a hug. This is what I needed. I feel the tension ease and relax into her, holding on tight. "Thank you for coming."

She pulls back and gives me a warm look. "Always Jules, remember."

With a nod, I recall our childhood promise to always be there for one another, and we have. I take Sam's hand, and we sit on the couch while I tell her everything. I'm not leaving any detail out, and it feels so good to say it out loud. Not just the night's events, but my inner thoughts and why I think I dated him to begin with. It wasn't just attraction; part of it was my need for companionship.

To my surprise, Sam squeezed my hand and smiled, but it was sad. "I feel that way too sometimes, Jules. But I'm not doing the bar or club thing. It's not me. I guess I believe the right guy will come along one day."

Maybe she's right. Me meeting guys in bars on Friday nights hoping one of them will be Mr. Right isn't working. All I meet are assholes. "I never want to see him again." I stare her in the eyes so she can see my determination.

Sam nods, her expression turns fierce, and that has my stomach in knots. She has a crazy streak. Hell, as teenagers, even her Uncle Fred called her that after the stunt she pulled. "You don't have to. You deserve someone who treats you with the respect and love you deserve." Sam's words are so sweet but don't match her expression.

We talk a little while longer before she leaves, and I can't shake this nagging feeling that something will happen. Seeing it's already after 9 p.m. I decide to lock up and go to bed. Tomorrow is a brand new day, and I refuse to let what Steve did define me. I won't stop wishing for Mr. Right and won't feel powerless. I swipe the stray tear that escaped and climb into bed, knowing tomorrow will be better.

Chapter 3

Sam

All the emotions I pushed down deep seeing Jules' face, knowing that the prick touched her, are now raging. I let them boil up and embrace them as I pull out of her driveway. He thinks he can touch her and get away with it. A malicious laugh bubbles out of me as I drive slowly until I get a few blocks away so I don't alert Jules to what I'm doing. Once I'm far enough away, I slam the peddle to the floor, and my head jerks back against the headrest. The roar of the 427 under the hood has my blood pumping.

Reaching into my back pocket, I slide my phone out and hit speed dial for Uncle Fred. The man knows shit; he has an ear to the ground, as they say. If anything happens on the Southside, he knows. Hell, maybe the entire city.

Uncle Fred picks up on the third ring with a groggy voice. Shit, I didn't think about him being asleep. He's usually drinking with Roger on Friday nights. "Sorry to wake you."

He clears his throat, and I feel terrible for calling, but I need information. "What's going on?"

I grip the steering wheel tighter and grit the words out. "Something happened, and I need to know Steve's hangouts."

I hear covers rustling, knowing he's sitting up now. "Steve, as in the little shit Jules has been dating?"

"Ya, he laid hands on her." As soon as the words are out of my mouth, I hear something crash on his end of the line. "Uncle Fred, I'll deal with him. Just tell me what you know."

"Sam, you're not going alone. Who knows who will be with him?" He sighs, then continues. "Have you heard of a place on the north side called Club Lust?"

"Ya, it opened last month." I grind my teeth, thinking I should've known. The wealthy crowd always flocks to the newest hottest clubs.

I hear Uncle Fred moving around and wait for anything else he can tell me as I weave furiously through the streets toward the north side. "Well, when she started seeing Steve, I asked around. That's where he and his crowd go. I'll meet you there."

"Love you," I say, knowing there is no arguing with him. If he wants to watch the show and have my back, so be it. I hit the end call button and tossed my phone into the passenger seat. Heading straight for the strip, horns blare as I weave in and out of traffic, cutting a few people off.

Grasping the shifter, I throw it down into third, hit the brakes, and jerk the wheel, making the tires squeal around the turn leading to the strip. I floor the gas peddle again, and the engine thunders down the road. "Steve, you're about to have a night to remember." A familiar fire burns in my stomach, and I push it down until I have him in my sights.

I slow down as I pass by the high rises coming to Club Lust. Their parking lot is overflowing with vehicles. I drive around for 10 minutes, looking for his red Porche. When I spot it, I grin and park crossways, blocking him in. Popping the glove compartment open, I take out the taser Roger got me, leaving the Mace where it is. However, I grab the 9mm and tuck it in the back of my jeans, not knowing what I'll run into inside.

Slamming my door harder than intended on my baby, I murmur an apology as I storm away towards the entrance. Walking up to the bouncers at the door, they give me a slow perusal. Clearly, I'm not dressed for clubbing. I still have on my grey work shirt with my name on the left breast, blue jeans, and steel-toed boots because, one time, dropping a torque wrench on my foot was enough. I flash them a wide smile and tilt my head to the side sweetly. They side-eye each other. "You here to look at the beer cooler?"

So they think I'm a repairman? I internally roll my eyes at how stupid. I'm wearing my work clothes, but seriously don't repairmen carry tools? Deciding to play along, I grin. "Sure." They shrug and let me pass.

I stop once inside and scan the club. Multi-colored lights in hues of red and blue swirl above a massive dance floor, music is booming, and bodies grind. A bar lines the left wall, and tables surround the rest of the room. I look up and see a balcony with private tables and a glass room dead center. Security or private offices? I don't know; and don't care. I slide the Taser from my waistband where I hid it and grip it tight as I slowly make my way through sweaty, grinding

LUST AND BLOOD

bodies. Halfway around the dance floor, I spot a male figure that catches my eye. A man that looks like Steve is sucking face with a young blonde in a short red dress. Well, he moved on fast. I turn sideways, squeezing through the crowd, getting closer, and he tilts his head to kiss her deeper. Giving me a perfect side view of his face. Yep, that's fucking Steve. I grip the Taser tighter and walk up behind him. Fisting the back of his hair, I jerk his head back forcefully. While simultaneously planting the Taser in his lower back and lighting him up. A long, continuous scream rips from him as he jerks violently. The pretty blonde screams and people step back. I release the trigger on the Taser and watch him fall to his knees, but I don't release his hair. Leaning down so my mouth is beside his ear, so he hears every word. "Stay the fuck away from Jules. And never fucking hit a woman." I enunciate every word before standing straight again. Steve takes a few deep breaths and turns to see who I am, and his eyes widen. I smirk at him, then slam the butt end of the Taser down on the bridge of his nose, breaking it, then turn, walking away.

If he thinks I'm done with his punishment, he's wrong. He touched something I love, so I'll return the favor. As I exit the club, the crowd parts for me, and bouncers look from me to upstairs stepping in my path. Well, so much for a quick exit.

"I think the boss wants to speak with you." The middle one says and I cock a brow.

"You think he does?" Tilting my head to the side, studying him.

His lip twitches slightly, and he gestures towards an elevator I hadn't noticed before. "Please come with us."

"Does your boss have two legs?" I ask with a deadpan face, knowing I'm pushing my luck. Everyone knows who owns this place. The same brothers who own half the city, the Rizzo's. They call them the blood kings because they rule with an iron fist.

He nods with a smirk. "He does."

"Then he can come find me if he wants to talk." I show him my brightest smile and walk around them, hoping like hell they just let me pass without making a scene. I'm a woman on a mission.

Once back at my car, I toss the Taser inside. Pulling my keys, I pop the trunk on my 67 Camaro and retrieve my trusty crowbar. So many uses, so little time, I think and chuckle, walking over to Steve's Porche.

It's such a shame you got stuck with him as an owner, I think, pulling back and swinging with all my might. Smash! His windshield's screwed. Crash! The driver's window shattered. That took 3 hits. Maybe I need to work out. Walking around, I do the passenger window. I glimpse movement and see Uncle Fred standing with a broad grin, feet planted firmly and arms crossed, watching me. I hear yelling in the distance but ignore it as I walk around the car, making sure I royally fuck up every quarter panel and the hood.

Uncle Fred's voice pulls me out of my head and fun when he yells into Steve's face. I guess he wanted to watch me redecorate his car. You deserve worse than this, so watch and learn, boy. I smile at Steve when I see blood all over his face and shirt. Swinging the crowbar again, I smash each headlight before I turn towards him, seeing Uncle Fred holding him back. "Remember what I said, Steve, stay away. You so much as breathe Jules' name, and I'll pay you a visit again."

His lip curls and his eyes bore into mine. "Bitch," he says through clenched teeth, and I chuckle.

With a shake of my head, I meet his stare. "You have no idea. But fuck with someone I love again, and you'll find out." I toss the crowbar into the trunk, shutting it.

Uncle Fred pulls me into a hug, kissing my forehead. "My crazy Sam."

I laugh, squeezing him around the waist. "Learned from the best." I grin when I see his Roadrunner parked a little way down the aisle of cars. "Brought the old girl out of the garage, I see."

"Yep, I couldn't leave you hanging. Made it here in record time."

We both get into our cars and fire them up. The small crowd is now more interested in the two muscle cars rumbling and the raw power they exude than the show I put on. With a smile, I grab the shifter, ease the clutch out, and roll down the row of cars. I'm sure they expected me to peel out of here, but why do the expected? Pulling onto the road, I see Steve fuming mad watching us leave. I roll down my window, raise my arm up high, and fly the bird before flooring it.

Chapter 4

Luca

I stand from my desk, rolling my stiff shoulders, and go to the bar. It's been a long fucking day. Pouring two fingers of whiskey, I walk over to the glass overlooking the club. As I survey the writhing bodies on the dance floor, I can hear the dull beat of the music pumping. We've had a packed house every weekend since we opened. Marcus was a genius at picking this location and hiring an amazing decorator.

Looking around the crowd, I stop mid-drink when I see the most gorgeous creature walk in I've ever seen. A mass of dark hair piled on her head, a grey button-up that doesn't hide her firm perky tits, tight jeans that hug every damn curve, down to black boots. I let my gaze roam back up her body, noticing that the shirt makes me think she just came from work. She's not dressed for clubbing.

Seeing her head turn, scanning the crowd, I take in her facial features. Tanned sun-kissed skin. I can't make out her eye color, but I see the wild look on her expression. This club's full of people looking to have fun or get laid. Not her. She looks ready to hurt someone.

I pull my phone to alert security to watch, but not intervene unless I say different. Stepping closer to the glass, I can't take my eyes off her as she weaves in and out of the grinding bodies below. She stops towards the back of the dance floor and zeros in on a couple, making my jaw clench. Is he her boyfriend? I want her; I think as my dick presses firmly against my zipper.

Her hand goes to her waist, then I see a glint of metal and sit my glass down. I'm torn between watching what she does next and running downstairs. I can't pull my eyes away as she walks up, grabs his hair, and tasers the fuck out of him. A dark chuckle erupts from my chest, watching him shake violently until he falls to his knees.

The goddess bends down, saying something to him before smashing his nose. I chuckle at the sight unfolding below and slide my hands into my pockets. When she stands straight and walks away like a fucking queen, my dick jerks to full mass. "Who are you?"

Pulling my phone back out, I dial our underboss Lou to have her followed but not touched. I need to know everything. "You got it, boss," Lou replies.

I walk over to the security monitors, pulling up the parking lot cameras. Spotting her on the east side of the building, I zoom in. I continue chuckling as I watch the scene unfold. Her smashing his car, what looked like a warning from an older man holding him back, forcing him to watch, while she did it. Fuck, I need to know her. Have her in my bed, in my life.

When she leaves, I watch closely, ensuring our men tail them. "Soon, mia regina," I say. (My Queen) Going to my desk, I isolate the time frame she was here and send a copy to Marco, then sit back, staring at the door, sipping my drink.

As I expected, he was through the door in less than 20 minutes. Long enough for him to watch it. "Who is she?"

I laugh at his reaction. We've had the same taste in women as long as I can remember. I knew that video would rile him up. "I have men on it. With any luck, we'll know everything by morning."

Marco's jaw ticks, and he pours himself a drink before returning. I don't miss the erection he's sporting when he sits. Watching her in action had an intense physical effect on him as well.

He takes a slow drink, then balances the glass on his thigh with a grin. "She royally fucked up that Porche."

"She did. It was fantastic to watch." I lean forward, resting my arms on the desk, watching him.

Marco locks eyes with me, and his expression is serious.

"Get information on the older man that was with her. We need everything." I nod in understanding. Although we rule the family together, Marco is the brain, whereas I am the muscle. I much prefer cracking heads to dealing with the business side of things.

"Done," I say, leaning back in my chair. Lou always goes above and beyond when we give him an order. He'll get us everything we need on both.

LUST AND BLOOD

Marco smirks at me with a gleam in his eye. "We both want her." It's something we've encountered before, but this feels different. This isn't some woman we each fuck and show the door. I want to know her.

I meet Marco's serious expression with my own. "Yes, but this is different."

He nods in agreement. "She carries herself like a queen. I need to know more."

I grin, leaning back. "That's what I immediately thought. How do we handle this?"

Marco looks down at his glass, circling the bottom of it on his thigh in deep thought. "We do something we've never done before. Get to know her, ask her out."

When his eyes meet mine again, I know he can see my tense expression. Neither of us has dated before. Fuck, I'm 26 and he's 28. Never once have either of us done more than buy a drink for a woman before we fucked her and sent her on her way. Marco chuckles at me before tossing back the rest of his drink. "You're thinking about the minor issues. I'm more concerned about the big picture."

I raise a brow, wondering what the fuck he's talking about. "One, we have both had the same women in the past, but not shared at the same time. Two, getting her to date and accept both of us."

I pinch the bridge of my nose and mutter a fuck before meeting his gaze. "Not an issue sharing we're family. But we'll have to convince her. I've been hard since she was here." There's no need to continue because he knows the rest. I won't stop until I have her. Hell, I want more than a taste; no way one night will satisfy me.

We talk business and discuss the upcoming meeting with the Romano's until close to midnight when there's a knock on the door. "Enter," Marco says.

Lou comes in carrying two files and gives them to Marco. I wait patiently while he reads through the first one before handing it to me. Opening it, I read through everything carefully.

Samantha Simms, goes by Sam, is 24 years old. She's worked at Gearhead Custom's on the Southside since she was a teenager. "Sam." I carry on reading as her name rolls off my tongue.

She has a 69' Camaro 427 Rock Crusher 4 speed registered in her name. The only vehicle listed. I smile, recalling her getting into it before leaving. She has good taste in cars. While I keep reading, my eyebrows furrow. Her best friend, Jules, also works at the garage.

Sam lives above Gearhead's in an apartment, and her Uncle Fred raised her. It was probably him with her outside the club. Why did he raise her? "Where's the rest of her family?"

I stare at Lou, waiting for an answer, but he points to Marco. Marco closes the file and clenches his jaw so hard I'm surprised he hasn't cracked a tooth. His eyes meet mine, and I wait for him to explain what's in his file.

My patience is wearing thin while he pours us both a drink, then tells Lou to leave us. Once he sits, I take a drink, knowing I'll need it. Marco leans back in his chair, staring at me for several minutes before speaking. "They died in a house fire when she was 6. Her uncle Fred was spending the weekend with them. He got Sam out but couldn't go back inside to get his sister or her husband before the house was engulfed in flames. The report says that you could hear their screams from outside while they burned alive." He shakes his head with a pained look.

I take a long drink, slamming my glass down on the desk. Fuck, I can't imagine seeing and hearing that as a child.

My stomach is in knots as Marco continues to speak. "By the time the fire department arrived, there wasn't much left. Her uncle raised Sam as his own after that moving out of the small apartment above his garage and buying a 2 bedroom home. Where Sam grew up next door to Jules."

I lean my head back, staring at the ceiling, thinking over what my queen has been through. Her only family is an uncle and her friend, Jules. "Change that," a voice in my head echoes, making my chest tighten. That's exactly what I plan on doing.

Marco stares at me with a knowing look when I sit straight again. We'll be her family. She will be ours. "Tomorrow." It's the only word I need to say.

Marco gives me a firm nod, standing. "Let's call it a night, brother. Lou can handle things."

I shut my computer down and we take the elevator upstairs to the penthouse. We both exit the elevator, going our separate ways to our rooms.

Without conscious thought, I do my normal routine: removing my jacket, laying it on the back of the chair in the corner before sitting to take my shoes off. When I stand, my eyes land on the king bed. I've never given it much

LUST AND BLOOD

thought, but we've never brought a woman home. Even before we moved into the penthouse above the club, we never wanted them to get the wrong idea. But Sam, I want her here, in my life, in my bed.

Chapter 5

Sam

Today will be interesting, I think to myself. Knowing someone will bring up last night, I'm not sure how Jules will react when she hears what I did. She worries about me and how out of control I am sometimes, but she doesn't need to. I shake my head, knowing I need to get my head into work before going downstairs.

Screwing the lid on my travel mug, I make my way down and see Jules, Roger, and Uncle Fred in the breakroom talking. I look at each of them, and they give me knowing looks. "Guess the cat's out of the bag."

Jules gets a mischievous grin, and Roger smirks. "What?"

Roger leans forward, eyes sparkling. "You're a little wildcat."

"She's crazy," Jules says. "But I love her for it." She stands, throwing her arms around my neck, making me laugh.

Looking at Uncle Fred, who has a broad grin, I raise an eyebrow, and he shrugs.

I sigh and step back from Jules. "He needed to be taught a lesson. It was perfect that a woman gave it to him." Uncle Fred's eyes crinkle at the corners as he laughs over the rim of his cup. I'm sure he recalls how pathetic Steve was last night.

We all eat donuts and drink our morning coffee until time to open. God, I love my little family. We may not all be blood, but we're family. Standing, I refill my coffee mug before we all go our separate ways to start our day.

We've worked together for so long that things run smooth as silk here. I sit at my desk, boot the computer, and pull this week's schedule to review. Not seeing my pen, I open the center desk drawer to grab one and my eyes land on the small two-inch picture of my parents I keep tucked away.

Sadness rolls through me before the sounds of their screams fill my head. I slam the drawer closed and squeeze my eyes shut, begging them to stop.

I hear three raps on my door and open my eyes, seeing Jules with a folder. "You're remembering, aren't you?"

I nod and take a deep breath, trying to hold off the tears. "Sometimes I wish I could forget, even if that meant forgetting them. Does that make me a horrible person?" My voice is barely above a whisper.

Jules rushes forward, slamming the file on my desk, and takes my hand. "Sam, you're the best person I know. I can't imagine seeing what you and Roger did. I'd probably curl up in bed and never get out." She pauses, squeezing my hand tight. "If you ever want to talk, I'm here."

I smile and stand, hugging her. "Thanks Jules, but you don't need that shit in your head too. Nobody does." I haven't told her the details and won't. She's too sweet to hear about that night.

"There's a list of parts we need for the Grand Torino job," she says, pointing to the file she put on my desk. "You have an appointment in one hour."

I pick up the file and lean back, waiting for her to tell me about the customer. With a grin, Jules walks to the door and glances over her shoulder. "Mr. Rizzo called and said he wanted to discuss your activities in his club last night. I told him you'd be happy to meet with him."

I cock a brow. "You did what?"

Jules gives me a broad smile. "We both know who the Rizzo brothers are. Hot. You need a distraction today." She walks out, laughing all the way back to the front counter.

Fuck, what the hell could they want? It's not like I damaged their property. I shake it off and get to work. Whatever it is, I'll deal with it when they get here.

I must have lost track of time because it seemed like only minutes had passed before there's another knock on my door. Looking up, I see Jules grinning mischievously. She did a great job of covering the bruises I know are under her makeup. There's only a shadow below her lip, and the swelling is barely noticeable. Jules is dainty and beautiful, but has a playful mean streak, making me wonder what she's up to. "The Rizzo's are here."

"Escort them in," I say, leaning back in my chair. My stoic face is firmly in place, so I don't show my emotions. I run my thumb over the edge of the desk out of habit, knowing I have a gun just inside if I need it.

LUST AND BLOOD

She nods, stepping aside with an outstretched hand, gesturing inside my office. Then, I see two mouth-watering men walk in. The first is older, Marco. He's easily 6 foot 3 inches, with dark hair that's perfectly in place. He has brown eyes I could get lost in, with a well-defined jaw that's clean-shaven. My eyes trail lower over an expensive black suit with a white button-down that does nothing to hide his large pectoral muscles and biceps flexing. He's gorgeous.

My gaze goes to his brother. If I remember correctly, his name's Luca. He's an inch shorter, with dark hair, slight stubble on his jaw, and dark eyes. However, he's a couple of years younger. His dark suit has a black button-down underneath in contrast to his brothers. Shit, my nipples are getting hard. What the hell is wrong with me?

He clears his throat, and my eyes snap to his, seeing a smirk. I roll my eyes at him. Too bad I can't control the blush creeping up my face. The five-alarm blaze I'm feeling in my cheeks lets me know they have to be red.

I glance at Jules, who's trying to stifle a laugh, observing me.

Keeping a straight face is difficult, but I manage. "And what do we owe the pleasure of having the Rizzo brothers here at Gearheads?" I ask cooly, hoping to save myself from this embarrassment of eye fucking them.

They both take their time looking me over from the top of my head down to my breasts, pausing. My core aches, and I know my panties are wet. I need to control myself and get my game face on.

Jules clears her throat, getting my attention. "You might want to do something about that," Jules says, looking at me but pointing to her chin.

"What?" I ask with a raised brow.

"The drool," she says through a laugh.

"Bitch," I deadpan.

A large man who came with the Rizzo's steps closer to Jules. "What's your name, gorgeous?" he asks. Her cheeks flush pink, but her back straightens.

"I'm busy," is her reply. It's sassy, but she's obviously flustered.

"Hmm, feisty," he says. I'm trying my best not to laugh as her face reddens.

"I have to get back to work," Jules says, grabbing the door so he knows to move out of the way.

The large man with the Rizzo's walks away chuckling, the Rizzo's look amused, and Jules shuts my door. Turning my focus back to Marco and Luca, who are now looking at me. "Have a seat, gentlemen."

They both sit, unbuttoning their suit jackets as they do, and I have to press my thighs together. Placing both hands on my desk, I square my shoulders, eyeing them both. "What can I do for you?"

Marco's lip twitches, hiding a smile as he gets comfortable. Damn, I'd love to see that smile. "Seems you had an eventful night at our club last night."

I grin and meet his gaze head-on. "I did. Some justice needed to be served and the deserving person just happened to be at Club Lust."

His eyes go hard, and Luca sits straight, getting my attention. Our eyes lock, and I see the question coming before he asks. "What did this man do?"

I narrow my eyes as memories of how Jules looked last night. "He laid hands on Jules. I have a strict policy. Hurt my family, and I hurt you." I trace circles on the desk, watching his expression before continuing. "I'm sure you both understand the importance of protecting family." Looking from Luca to Marco.

"Are you always that passionate about things?" Luca says, making my eyes snap to him. His half grin tells me he's not just talking about my temper. He's flirting with me.

I tilt my head to the side and give him a slow smile. "Always." His eyes flash, and there's no mistaking the heat I see behind them.

They both have a gleam in their eyes, and Marco smirks at me. "Have dinner with us."

It's not really a question, and I'm stunned. This isn't at all what I expected. My traitorous body hums at the thought of going out with them. Them? Wait, he said us. I look between them and they both smile.

"Why would I go out with you?" The questions just comes out without thinking.

Lucas leans forward, resting his elbows on his thighs. "Because you want to."

Marco stands, buttoning his jacket, towering over my desk. "Because we want to know you, mia regina."

I swallow hard, staring at them. "I don't think that's a good idea."

Suddenly, my office door bursts open. "She would love to." An excited Jules stands there, smiling from ear to ear. Fuck, she's been eavesdropping this whole time? Her eyes bounce around the room before landing on me.

LUST AND BLOOD

"See, Jules agrees," Luca says with a smirk, standing beside his brother. With both of them now towering over me, I feel small.

Gathering myself, I push my chair back, standing as well. "Fine, name the place and time." What could one meal hurt?

Stepping closer, Marco looks down at me. My desk is between us, but it may as well not be. The raw power and dominance radiating off him and Luca permeates the air. "We'll pick you up at 6 p.m. tonight."

I shake my head no. No way am I riding with them. If anything goes wrong, I want my own transportation. "Name the place and time. I'll meet you." My voice is firm, and he can see my determination.

"Fine, Romano's at 6 p.m.," Marco says reluctantly.

I glance at Luca, who has now stepped closer. "Sam," my name on his lips has my body doing all kinds of things I don't recognize. "Don't keep us waiting."

I dig my fingers into the palms of my hands to gain control of whatever is happening to me. "I'm never late." My voice comes out calm, thankfully, and he gives me a firm nod and a smile before turning towards the door.

Jules shows them out, and I flop into my chair and think, What did I agree to? I'm out of my depth here. I don't do fancy restaurants and clubs. My idea of fun is cars, fighting, eating pizza, and drinking beer. I'm jerked out of my thoughts when Jules enters, and I give her the death glare.

She approaches, swaying her hips and wagging her index finger at me. "Don't do that. You need some fun, and those two..." she pauses, giving me a mischievous grin. "They look like a lot of fun."

I burst out laughing and lay my head back, staring at the ceiling. "Maybe, but Jules, I don't own anything to go out in. Shit, my idea of dressing up is jeans and a tank top without holes."

"I've got you covered. Just come over to my place after work," Jules says, and I raise my head, eyeing her.

"Ok, but nothing too crazy." My warning is clear. I've seen some dresses she wears out.

She tilts her head to the side, studying me. "Why are you so grumpy?"

The truth is the truth, so I blurt it out. "I'm horny and flustered."

Jules slaps her hand over her mouth, laughing, and I grunt in disapproval. She would enjoy my situation.

Chapter 6

Marco

The woman I now know as Jules gestures for us to enter Sam's office. I walk in, glancing around until my eyes land on a fucking goddess behind a desk. She does a slow perusal of me, making my pants become increasingly uncomfortable. I don't miss the desire in her eyes as she does it.

When her eyes shift to my brother, I resist the urge to adjust myself. She gives Luca the same lust-filled look as she takes him in. She may have a straight face, but her eyes give away her wants.

I watch and listen to her interaction with her friend. I always observe before speaking. It's practiced with those outside the family, but I don't want her to be an outsider. I want her. I chuckle lowly at their banter, then at the interaction between Lou and Jules. There's definite interest there. I don't miss the bruising that her friend is hiding behind that makeup, and I doubt Lou did, either.

When Sam tells us to sit, her eyes land back on me exactly where they belong. I want them focused on us always. When I hear Jules shut the door, I get comfortable, as much as possible, with the aching hard-on that's dying to be buried inside her.

Luca and I test the waters with light flirting, and she plays along. The more I hear her speak and watch how she carries herself, the more I know she's the one. The one I've been waiting for. Sam is the perfect woman for us. Now we just have to convince her to get to know us, so she sees it too.

When I ask her out to dinner, it wasn't really a question, and she recognized that. Good, I'm not a man who takes no for an answer. I always get what I want, and I want Sam. I do have to concede for now with her meeting us at Romano's, but with her, I'll have to learn some semblance of compromise. She's not one to hand over control without trust. I'll earn that trust.

"See you at 6, mia regina," I say under my breath, leaving her office. Luca doesn't miss it and side-eyes me with a smirk. He feels it, too; she's it. The mythical woman we didn't think existed. Fucking perfect, I feel it.

Walking through the showroom towards the exit, her friend Jules steps around the counter, blocking our path, and I stop raising a brow.

Jules puts her hand on her hip, meeting my gaze, which few people do. "I helped you out in there. Don't screw it up." I almost laugh when she looks between me and Luca with a hard look.

"Not a chance," Luca says, standing shoulder-to-shoulder with me. Jules nods before turning and going down the hall towards Sam's office with a proud look.

Taking my seat in the car, Lou looks at me through the rearview. "Make sure our private room is ready for 6 p.m."

Lou nods, pulls his phone out, and dials our restaurant. We rarely give the staff a heads-up when we're coming, but tonight's different. I want everything flawless for Sam.

I look over at Luca, who's smiling. "She's perfect."

He nods. "I didn't think I'd ever find the one, but brother, she's it."

We both feel it. It never crossed my mind we'd share the ideal woman, but here we are. I hope she's ready for us. Just as the thought passes through my mind, I see Luca adjusting himself. I follow the action, doing the same because, damn; I don't need a permanent impression of the zipper on my shaft.

We're almost back to the penthouse before Luca speaks again. "Do we need to talk about how we'll approach things with her tonight?"

I look at him and lay it out. "We want her. Not for a night, but long term."

"Yes, she's the one," he says with conviction.

I smirk, knowing that we both feel the same way. "She's ours, so we make her family. We get what we want. That's not changing now."

Luca stares out the window before returning his gaze to me. "We've both seen the tapes of last night and read her file. She's a fighter, but I don't want her fighting us on this. We move at her pace."

"I agree, brother. She has a lot of pent-up pain and lashes out. We build trust and make sure she knows this is permanent. We'll figure things out as we go," I say, leaning back and unbuttoning my jacket.

LUST AND BLOOD

Pulling up outside the club, I watch and listen as Luca pulls out his phone and has flowers delivered to the restaurant for tonight. Something I should have thought of. We enter the elevator, and I straighten my cufflinks before speaking. "It's good there's two of us. You thought of something I didn't. When that happens with one of us, the other can step in."

Luca's chest puffs out with pride before side-eyeing me. "Ya, you're the think tank. I'm sure I'll be the one who forgets things."

At five minutes to 6 p.m., Luca and I are standing inside the restaurant waiting for Sam's arrival. I don't want to miss a moment with her, so I'm not letting the staff escort her to our private room. I see movement out of the corner of my eye, and a low growl rumbles from my chest. Luca turns, seeing what I see.

A regular from the club who's always trying to get invited upstairs into VIP. She, as well as her little clique, has tried many times to get an introduction to us. I'm not interested and neither is Luca. I know her type well, wanting to land a rich boyfriend or husband.

She's brave walking up, tossing her long hair over her shoulder, and wearing a dress that's two sizes too small with her tits out. She's trying too hard to get noticed as she places her hand on my arm. I grab her wrist, removing it, and she laughs nervously. "Hello Mr. Rizzo, I'm surprised to see you here." Her voice is high-pitched, making my lips curl in disgust.

I glare down at her before speaking. "Seeing as how we own the restaurant and its public knowledge, I doubt that."

Shock flashes in her eyes before she masks it. My tone was harsh, hoping she would take the hint. But she isn't smart and still stands there looking at me.

"Excuse us while we escort our date inside," Luca says, saving her from my next words. They would have been much harder. I hate desperate women. She huffs as we walk away, making me grin.

Chapter 7

Sam

Soaking in the hot bath, I lean my head back, relaxing, letting all the stress of today leave me. I sink lower and begin washing my hair as my mind drifts.

Am I crazy for agreeing to dinner? I sigh, realizing that nothing can come of this. We live in two different worlds and there's two of them. With my past, I'm too messed up for dating games, and a fling has never interested me. I'll just make that clear to them.

I wash and rinse while I think of different conversation tactics. Once I'm dry, I wrap a towel around my body and enter the bedroom.

Jules is sitting in a chair at the vanity, smiling. I groan, walk over, and dread whatever she has picked out for me to wear. With a raised brow, I eye her carefully. "Well, where is it?"

She points to the bed, and I see a red dress. It's beautiful and looks long enough, but it's low cut. Deciding to see it on before giving her a piece of my mind. I drop the towel and slip it on. Walking to the mirror, I take it in. Running my hands over my stomach and hips, I can't help but smile. It hugs every curve and goes to just above my knees. I turn, seeing it makes my butt look great. The deep 'v' in the front has me concerned. I'm not one to wear revealing clothes. I have a slender body and a small C cup that fits my frame. With a grin, I turn and look at her. "Thanks, Jules, it's beautiful."

She stands with a proud look. "It's perfect on you."

"I love it, but maybe I should cancel." She laughs at me, shaking her head. "You could go with me and let the big guy with a thing for you buy you dinner."

Jules's face goes red, and she adamantly shakes her head. "No more bad boys for me. Besides, tonight's about you, woman." She points at me with a smirk before handing me a thong. I groan and rip the price tag from it before slipping it on under the dress. Jules irritates me most of the time with her cheerfulness, but I love her.

She exits the bedroom, and I sit at the vanity, blow-drying my hair. I decide to leave it down for once in long natural waves. Wearing it up every day, I forget how long it is. I stare into the mirror, seeing myself in a different light. The woman looking back at me isn't the grease monkey from the garage who does office work. I'm a woman going out on the town.

Looking around the room, I spot a pair of black stilettos next to the door and slip them on. I'm ready to go. Swaying my hips, I stroll into the living room, seeing Jules standing with her arms crossed, leaning against the kitchen counter.

She gives me a broad grin, looking me over carefully. "You look amazing."

"I always look good," I say, looking down and running my hand over my hip, smoothing the dress down. My stomach gets a knot in it, and I give Jules a serious look. "My gut is telling me this is a mistake. That something will go wrong tonight."

Jules walks closer, studying me. "You can handle a date, and you know it. Besides, do you want to be alone forever?"

I shake my head, no, knowing she's right. I'll keep my guard up just in case, but still try to have fun.

Who would have thought my first date would be with the notorious Rizzo brothers? I almost laugh at that. Nothing about our interaction in my office made me feel threatened, just horny as hell. I can deal with that when I get home tonight.

Looking back at Jules, I recall the last few days. "Are you staying in tonight?"

She nods and grins. "Yep, watching a movie and reheating some takeout. Have fun and don't worry about me."

I take her hand and whisper. "I just can't stand the thought of anything happening to you. If Steve or anyone were to hurt you again, I don't know what I would do."

Jules gives me a warm smile and embraces me in a tight hug. "Nothing's happening to me. Besides, I felt powerful when I kicked him out. For the first time, I think I channeled my inner Sam."

LUST AND BLOOD

I can't help the laughter that erupts from me. I squeeze her tight before pulling back, looking at her. "You have an inner Jules. It's about time she came out to play."

Walking back into the bedroom, I pull my keys and phone from my pants, seeing I still have cash in the case. With a nod, I palm them and turn, walking out. I've never carried a purse, always keeping a hundred in my phone case.

When I arrive at Romano's, the valet is immediately at my door, opening it. But he can't take his eyes off my car, admiring it. I step out and stare him down until his gaze meets mine. The young man's face goes stone straight when he sees my hard expression. Good. "There better not be a scratch on her when I get her back." My voice is low and firm. He doesn't miss the warning and gives me a nod.

I walk around him towards the entrance and see Marco and Luca exiting the restaurant, looking me over from head to toe. Warm butterflies fill my stomach, making me grin. I guess they like what they see by the lust in their eyes.

They each reach out a hand, taking mine. Tucking them into the crook of their arms, they escort me inside. An older man is waiting and leads the way towards a wide staircase. We pass by several tables of patrons, but one catches my eye in particular.

Three women dressed to the nines look me up and down with distaste and I stare them down. I'm the wrong woman to fuck with, and have never cared what others thought. We keep walking, and I put them out of my mind, determined to enjoy dinner.

We're led into a private dining room, and I feel relieved. I've never liked crowds.

There are three dining tables with linen cloths. I don't miss the dozen red roses sitting in the center of the middle table, and I look from Marco to Luca with a grin. Luca raises my hand, kissing the back, but his eyes never leave mine. "You deserve those, and so much more." I swear I feel like my heart will beat out of my chest.

Marco pulls on my other hand, turning me to face him. "If we have our way, this will be the first of many nights we spoil you." Did he really just say that? My guard instantly goes up because that shit sounds like a line he's said many times.

He pulls out my chair, and I sit, laying my phone on my lap. Willing myself to relax and study my surroundings. I've never been comfortable in strange places.

I lean back and meet each of their gazes. "Thank you for inviting me to dinner, gentlemen."

Marco gives me a sexy half smile, resting his hand on the table. "You're welcome, Sam." My name on his lips sends a shiver up my spine, and I try to hide it. Damn, why do they have to be so freaking handsome?

Luca leans over, so his mouth brushes against my ear. "You're more than welcome, mia regina." Shit, I need to get myself under control with these two.

I put my game face on and look into his eyes when he sits back. "What does mia regina mean?"

Luca gives me a slow smile. "I would rather show you before we tell you." Raising a brow, I decide if they want to flirt, I'll play along. Besides, I can already feel my panties getting wet. What's a little more flirting going to hurt?

Marco is observing Luca and me with a grin. I cross my ankles and rest my hands in my lap, waiting for their next move. It doesn't come because the waiter enters, placing water in front of us before opening a bottle of wine. I'm not a wine drinker at all. The stuff tastes like bad grape juice to me. "Beer please," I say before he pours it.

"You don't like wine?" Marco asks curiously.

"No, I prefer beer if I drink. Domestic beer preferably." I don't want to offend anyone, but I won't pretend to be someone I'm not.

Marco nods, snapping his fingers. "Get her a cold beer." The waiter jumps into action, and I have one in hand within minutes.

I take a drink and then look between them. Damn, they're gorgeous, and my nipples harden. Luca doesn't miss it either in this dress because the built-in bra doesn't hide it. I clear my throat, getting their attention. "Why did you ask me out?" The question is blunt, even for me and my big mouth. But I need to know. I'm not one to play games. I prefer direct and to the point.

Marco leans back and gives me a serious look. I know whatever he's going to say will hold the truth. "You're everything we ever wanted."

I almost choke on my spit. He's serious, dead serious, but there's one glaring truth he's not considering. "You don't even know me." The words just fly out of my mouth, but I don't regret them.

LUST AND BLOOD

"We know enough, and that's why we're dating. To get to know each other better. Beyond what we hear or read about one another," Luca says, gaining my attention. I'm stunned for a moment, and that never happens to me. He said we're dating. Like not in 'a' date but dating. I know what the public knows about them. But what have they heard or read about me? They're the fucking Rizzo's, meaning they probably did a background check. Fuck, they know about my past. My jaw clenches. Well, they think they know. No one knows the truth except Uncle Fred and me. Let it go, Sam, I chide myself.

"So, should I believe everything I read and hear about you?" I know the answer and so do they. I'm making a point here.

"No," Marco says before taking a drink of wine. I nod, turning to Luca, who is watching me.

I give him a smirk, making him grin. "What are you getting at?"

I shrug, picking up my beer. "Just making a point. Don't make assumptions based on what you read or hear."

Luca's facial expression changes, and he smiles. "Never, mia regina." He raises his hand, tracing a line from my bare shoulder down to the sensitive bend in my arm, leaving goosebumps in his wake. Shit, I need to get myself under control.

We place our orders, and Marco kisses my hand. "Why has such a beautiful creature as yourself been hiding in a garage?"

I smile at that because I know how most people react when they hear where I work. "Being raised by my ex-military uncle, certain things stuck. Early to rise, if you want something, work for it, and the garage went from my childhood playground to a place for me to earn money. I love what I do."

He nods with a genuine look of understanding. I'm sure he and Luca earned their positions the hard way. Luca takes a drink before sitting his glass down, watching us. "Do you always charge into situations that could get you harmed?"

Luca's tone is concerned, so I don't blow up at his words. I hate people who judge me and why I am the way I am. "That little prick couldn't beat himself off with both hands, more or less take me on. Therefore, I was in no danger."

Luca throws his head back and belts out a deep belly laugh. I chuckle lowly and look over at Marco, who is chuckling lowly. "You really are something, you know that?"

I shrug and grin. "So I've been told." My body relaxes, enjoying our fun banter until I realize I need to pee. Standing, I ask, "Where's the ladies' room?"

They both stand like the gentlemen they are and Marco points to the door. "Just across the hall is our private bathroom." I nod and thank him before making my way out.

After peeing, I exit the stall and wash my hands while admiring the luxurious bathroom through the mirror above the sink. I've never seen couches in a freaking bathroom before, but oh well. What ever floats their boat. The bathroom door opens and my eyes snap to the woman entering.

It's one of the women from down stairs earlier and I know damn well this is the Rizzo's private bathroom. There's only one reason she would be in here. She's wanting to speak to me.

I turn the water off and reach for a towel to dry my hands. But my eyes never leave her as she strolls towards me with a malicious grin. "It seems the Rizzo's are slumming it tonight. Such a shame when they deserve a woman with class by their side."

What the fuck did this bitch say? I drop the towel and turn on her. She pauses mid step, taking in my hard expression. I look her up and down slowly, curling my lip in disgust. "So your feelings are hurt because another woman has the attention of a man you want?" I eye her carefully and she looks like I slapped her. Tilting my head to the side, I decide to push further. "Or is it they fucked you and you just can't move on from the brush off?"

That did it. She's furious. She gasps and her face turns beat red before she charges me with a raised hand. I grab her wrist, swing her around, slamming her face into the wall. Pinning it there with my other hand. I chuckle, seeing her face squashed against it.

Leaning in close, I whisper just to piss her off. "Or is it that their wallets are more attractive than their dicks to you?" Her lack of response tells me everything I need to know. That my words hold some truth.

I push harder on her head, smashing her face further. "Let me educate you on something. You might be queen shit among your little group downstairs. But me, I'm more of a take the bull by the horns and fuck things up kinda woman. If you haven't figured it out yet, this isn't your day and I'm not the person to fuck with."

LUST AND BLOOD

I fist her hair, pulling her away from the wall before shoving her towards the door. "Now leave before I really mess up that pretty face of yours." She rushes to the door, jerking it open with tears running down her cheeks.

I shake my head at how pathetic some women are before picking my phone up off the side of the sink and leaving. As soon as I step into the hallway, I see Marco and Luca standing there, staring at me. They both have a million questions behind their eyes, and I sigh. "We were worried you were gone awhile," Marco says.

"Ya, well, it seems I needed to have a chat with one of your conquests," I say, harsher than intended.

Marco shakes his head no, and Luca steps close. "What happened?"

I meet his gaze with determination. "It doesn't matter. If that's the kind of woman you're used to dating, you need to go right back to them. I'm not interested." Knowing damn well if they touched her, I'll never let them lay a finger on me. Yuck.

Before I can step around them, I'm picked up off my feet, in the bathroom again and pinned to the wall. I fist Luca's shirt hard, ready to act on instinct, until he cups my face, putting his right in mine. "We've never touched her. You're the only woman we're interested in." His eyes are fierce, and I can feel the truth of his words. I nod but say nothing.

Luca kisses my forehead, lingering a moment before releasing me. Marcus steps close, towering over me, and takes my chin between his fingers. His eyes hold so many emotions as he stares down at me. "If you need time to see how serious we are about you, we'll give you that mia regina. What we won't give you is space. You're ours. I know you feel it too. Everything about you pulls us in like a magnet. I'm not fighting it, and we won't let you."

I nod, not wanting to fight it. But I need time to know I'm not just a fling. I need to know them better. "We get to know each other."

Marco smiles, leans down, and kisses my cheek before releasing my chin. "Time," he says, stepping back.

My phone rings, getting my attention, and I see Jules's name on the screen. Is she calling to check up on me? I hold up a finger to Marco and Luca before answering. "Hey Jules. What's up?" Her frantic voice over the line has me on alert.

Chapter 8

Luca

Sam's entire body goes rigid, and she gets the eyes of a killer after answering the phone. I know that look. It stares back at me every time I look in the mirror. Something's wrong, and she's going to handle it. Probably kill whoever fucked up.

I clench my jaw tight, waiting and watching her expression. Marco steps closer to Sam, as ready as me to step in and take care of whatever has upset our woman. Listening closely, I hear an upset Jules say a name, Steve. Then I catch part of the conversation. "He's outside trying to get in."

Sam's face contorts in rage, then she kicks her heals off. "Keep the doors locked. I'm on my way." Before I know it, Sam pushes past us and runs full speed down the corridor, taking the steps two at a time. We're right behind her, prepared to end the fucker.

We pass through the dining room in a blur, but I catch sight of Lou and his crew at a table. "Backup now," I say, passing.

They're up and behind us without hesitation. Marco grabs Sam by the arm as she reaches the valet. "Get my car now." The valet's eyes go wide, but he leaves immediately to retrieve it as Marco spins her around.

"What's happening? Talk to us." Marco's voice is firm, leaving no room for argument. I crowd close, so Sam knows we're here for her. She needs to realize we are in this for the long haul. We'll have her back, fuck we'll handle whatever it is for her.

Sam's chest heaves, studying our faces, but she relents. "Jules needs me now. The asshole didn't learn his lesson and is trying to break in."

That's all I need to hear. Jules is important to Sam, which makes her important to me. I look at the other valet, and he nods, grabbing our keys. As the owners, our vehicles are close. Our SUV arrives at the same time as Sam's. I grit my teeth when she runs getting into hers instead of riding with us. She has it in gear and moving before the driver's door fully closes, making me growl.

Marco jumps in the driver's seat of the SUV, and I'm in the passenger, immediately sliding my Glock out of my waistband, ready to end this fucker for upsetting Sam and interrupting our date. I brace a hand on the dashboard as we peel out of the parking lot and begin weaving through traffic. We whizz past cars while the sound of horns blaring fills my ears. I ignore it all, focusing solely on Sam's Camaro up ahead, which we are quickly losing. What the fuck has she done to modify that engine?

She's barely in sight when Marco curses, seeing what I do. The car goes sideways, taking a turn, running a red light, entering the south side, and the tires of her car smoke. I chuckle, leaning my shoulder into the door for support. "She'd be a great get-a-way driver."

Marco gives me a quick, hard look before focusing on the road. We're swerving in and out of cars. Everything is a blur. I know what he's thinking. She's strong but also careless, running into situations. My hand tightens around my gun, knowing I won't let anything happen to her.

To my shock, when we pull in behind her car, she is already out of it, charging up the porch of a small house with a gun drawn. "Fuck," I yell, jumping out and running. No way is she going inside alone. Marco jumps out of the SUV and is beside me in a flash.

Charging through the door, everything seems to move in slow motion. The same man from the club grabs Jules by the hair. She swings a lamp, hitting him in the head. He stumbles back, then pulls a gun. I raise mine, and so does Marco. He's a dead man.

I hear two rapid shots and his body jerking as I pull the trigger. My mind doesn't register that Sam fired first until my eyes flick to her. She's standing with her feet apart and shoulders square. It's like seeing a fucking goddess in action.

When Steve's body drops to the floor, she takes two steps forward, and I match her, staying at her side. Sam raised her gun and fire's one last shot to the head and the light in his eyes instantly fades. I've seen it many times; he's dead.

Jules immediately embraces Sam. "Thank you for coming."

Sam wraps her arms around Jules, holding her. When her eyes lock on mine over Jules' shoulder, I see it. These two aren't just friends. They're family. We will protect them both.

LUST AND BLOOD

I'm pulled from my thoughts when two men burst through the back door of the house, guns drawn. Marco and I raise our guns until we see who it is. We saw them at the garage, and I instantly knew one of them was Sam's Uncle Fred, who raised her.

We all lower our guns, but both men are eyeing Marco and me carefully. When recognition of who we are crosses his face, he focuses back on Sam and Jules. "Are you two ok?"

Sam release Jules and steps into the biggest man's arms, making my fist clench. "We're fine Uncle Fred." I relax, reminding myself he's related to her. Jules assures Roger she's fine.

Instinctively, I step closer to Sam, wanting to be the one to comfort her if she needs it. Our men who were following us entered, finally arriving. I guess we need to talk to them about their lack of driving skills. While Sam explains to her uncle and Roger what happened, I tell our men to clean up the body and dispose of Steve's car.

After we're formally introduced to Uncle Fred and Roger, Marco says what I was thinking. "We looked into Steve after the club incident. His family's wealthy and influential. His disappearance won't go unnoticed. You two need to pack a bag and lie low for a while. Let us handle things."

Sam turns, glancing at us. "And where are we supposed to stay?"

I smirk stepping toe to toe with her and stroke her cheek. "With us, of course."

Sam flushes and her pupils dilate, letting me know she's aroused by the idea.

She pulls back to my disappointment when her uncle speaks. "They're right, Sam. If you're with the Rizzo brothers, no one will be able to touch you, including the police. Being with them is the smart move."

Sam hugs her uncle before stepping back and giving him a hard look. "Don't screw up the books while I'm gone," then she points at him, making me smile. "If that developer gives you any trouble, you call me."

Uncle Fred's lip twitches in amusement before replying. "I've handled men worse than him since before you were born. Don't worry about me."

I hear Roger mutter under his breath, "Hell cat," and Sam jerks her head in his direction.

Jules covers her mouth, laughing at them before walking away. In less than five minutes, she's back with a duffle bag that probably only holds a few days' clothes. I smirk, thinking Sam better pack a lot more than that, because if I have my way, she's never leaving our penthouse.

I take her hand in mine, gaining her attention. Let's get you packed. She nods, and we walk out, Marco taking her other hand. Sam pulls us towards her car. "What are you doing?"

Pausing at the door, Sam looks up at me. "Where I go, my car goes." Her expression says there's no arguing, so I don't. I take her keys, much to her disapproval, and escort her around to the driver's side, where Marco is holding the door open. I can tell he isn't happy about us riding separately, but we'll do anything for her.

After we have her and Jules safely inside, I enter the driver's seat, glancing in the rear-view mirror. Marco is in the SUV, ready to follow. "Buckle up, hellcat," I say. Sam's head jerks my way with a raised brow, and I smirk, starting the car. When it roars to life, and the deep rumble has my ass vibrating in the seat, I cock an eyebrow staring at her.

Sam grins at me, mischievously leaning her head back against the headrest. "Purrs like a kitten," she says and Jules's laughter rings out from the back seat. I shake my head, putting it into first, and take off like I own it. Because I will. I'll own every inch of Sam and all she loves if it's the last thing I do.

When we arrive at Sam's apartment above the garage, the women go into her room to pack, and I turn to Marco. "Who's room are we putting her in?"

He stares at me, contemplating how we decide, because there's no doubt she's sleeping with us. "Flip on it."

I slide my hand into my pocket, pulling out a quarter. "Heads or tails?" I ask with a smirk.

Marco grins, calling heads, and I nod, happy with that. I've always been an ass man, so tails suits me fine. I toss, catch, and then slap it in my palm before revealing it. "Tails it is."

Marco's eyes flash, knowing he'll have to carry his shit into my room. We agreed to share, not pass her back and forth. That means every night she'll be between us. We warned her she could have time but not space. She's about to find out what that means.

"I'm driving them back," Marco says, pulling me from my thoughts. I nod, knowing that's only fair since I drove them here. My chest tightens at the thought of being away from her, and one thing's certain. As soon as things

LUST AND BLOOD

settle, she's never leaving our side. This is more than want. I'm fucking falling for her. I've never been possessive or obsessed with a woman until Sam.

When they exit her bedroom, each carrying a suitcase, I step forward, taking it. Sam's eyes meet mine, and I see gratitude and longing. Does she know how badly I want to have her in my arms? To taste her lips with mine?

My eyes go to her mouth, and I unconsciously lick my lips. The thought of how sweet she would taste makes my mouth water. Her beautiful eyes reflect the same desire I feel when I look back at them. She wants me.

Raising my hand, I stroke over her jawline with my thumb. "Soon, hellcat."

Chapter 9

Marco

I glance around the penthouse as Luca finishes ordering Italian takeout for dinner. It's the first time Sam and Jules have seen our home. It's important that Sam likes it because it will be her home. We've only been here five minutes, and already the place feels different. More alive.

"Marco, where are our rooms?" Jules asks, her eyes wide with excitement.

"Follow me," I say, grabbing their suitcases and leading them down the hallway. I stop at the first door on the left. "Jules, this one's yours. And Sam, yours is right over here."

They peek inside, their faces lighting up as they take in the spacious rooms. "Wow, Marco, these are amazing!" Jules exclaims.

"Wait until you see the rest. Come on, I'll give you a tour," I say, taking Sam's hand in mine. The need to be close to her and feel her skin is overwhelming.

I guide them through the penthouse, pointing out the living room with its floor-to-ceiling windows. We pass through the living room into the dining room. As we enter, Luca is setting the table.

Jules and Sam immediately join in, helping him arrange the plates and cutlery. I instinctively rub my chest, seeing Sam in our home. She's everything I've ever wanted in a woman. So beautiful, smart, and fierce. Having her here feels right.

I head to the kitchen, grabbing a bottle of red wine and a beer for Sam. Remembering from the restaurant that she doesn't like wine. Opening both, I set them on the table just as the food arrives.

"Dinner's here," I announce, and we all take our seats. I guide Sam to sit beside me, while Luca takes the seat on her other side, leaving Jules across from her.

The aroma of Italian food mingles in the air with laughter and conversation. We serve ourselves. The clinking of utensils is a comforting sound.

"This place is incredible," Jules says, her eyes wide as she looks around.

Sam laughs, her eyes sparkling with amusement. "Jules, you act like you've never seen an apartment before."

"Not one like this," Jules says, and I can't help but chuckle.

My mind drifts to earlier when Sam ran into the house without us. "You should've waited for us, Sam," I say. My tone came out harsher than I intended. I soften my tone before continuing. "Running into that house ahead of us was reckless."

Her eyes snap to mine with a serious expression. "I'm used to handling things on my own, Marco. It's what I've always done."

Luca and I exchange a glance, realizing she's not used to someone having her back all the time.

The room goes quiet for several minutes until Jules breaks the silence in a playful tone. "Well, you've got Marco and Luca now, Sam. You're stuck with them."

Sam's lips curve into a smile. "Is that so?" It is, but I don't say that. Sam will soon find out that Luca and I aren't going anywhere, and neither is she.

We resume eating, and the mood feels lighter again. Jules leans forward, a mischievous glint in her eye. "I've got a crazy story from when Sam and I were kids..."

"Jules, behave," Sam warns in a firm voice. "Or I'll share some embarrassing stories about you."

I stand, gathering plates and carrying them to the kitchen. "I'm turning in early tonight," I announce. "Long day tomorrow."

Luca joins me, and together we clear the table and start washing the dishes. Sam and Jules follow, helping us finish the cleanup. Once everything's put away, we watch as they head to their rooms down the hall.

Luca and I move towards the bar in the living room. He pours us each a drink, and we sit in silence for a while, lost in our thoughts.

"Sam's the one," Luca says quietly, breaking the silence.

"She is," I agree. "We promised her time, but not space. She'll never sleep alone again."

LUST AND BLOOD

Luca nods with a determined look. "We'll give her thirty minutes to get ready for bed. Then we go in and tell her how things will be."

I raise my glass to that before taking a long drink. My body relaxes back into the couch, thinking of her. Sam is ours, and tonight we'll make sure she knows it.

Thirty minutes later, we make our way to Sam's room. The soft glow of the bathroom light filters into the bedroom, casting a gentle light on her figure lying in bed. She's covered by a sheet, her dark hair splayed out on the pillow, and her tanned skin glowing in the dim light.

When I shut the door behind us, she raises her head, looking at us. The sheet drops to her perfect mounds, drawing my eyes to them. "What are you doing in here?"

I let my eyes roam over her, taking in every detail. "We're here to claim what's ours," I say, in a low voice.

Luca moves to one side of the bed, and I take the other, slowly undressing and dropping our clothes to the floor. "Lie back down," I instruct her. "You need sleep after the day you've had."

Sam's eyebrows furrow, but she lies her head back on the pillow.

We slide under the covers, our bodies molding to hers. Sam's warmth seeps into me, making me aroused. Luca nuzzles into her hair, inhaling her scent and he groans. "Sleep well," he says into her hair.

Sam wiggles, trying to get comfortable, but her movements only intensify my arousal. The feel of her body against mine, the softness of her skin, has my shaft going from half mass to fully erect. I can feel pre-cum leaking onto my stomach. The ache to be inside her and claim her as mine, as ours, is intense.

I lean in, brushing my lips over her ear. "Do you need something, Sam?"

Her breath hitches, giving away the want she's feeling. "Yes," she whispers on an exhale.

I lift the sheet slightly and move over her, pinning her body down with mine. "Luca, take good care of her breasts," I command, running my hands down her body, realizing she's completely naked. "Fuck."

Luca captures her lips in a deep, demanding kiss while I trail my tongue and lips down her stomach to her core. Her scent is intoxicating. When I take that first long lick, her taste erupts on my taste buds. She's mouthwatering and

I can't get enough. Luca alternates between her breasts, his mouth and hands working in tandem.

When I begin eating her in earnest, devouring her pussy, she twists and groans our names, making my dick ache with need.

Sam's moans fill the room, and I see her hand wrap around Luca's cock, pulling it free from his briefs. "Cum on my breasts," she instructs him, her voice coming out breathy.

Luca takes her hand and they stroke his length together. I pick up my pace, making her legs shake. When I suck her clit into my mouth and flick it hard with my tongue, she jerks him hard. He releases with a yell, fisting her hair and coating her breasts as I continue eating my new favorite meal. Her orgasm hits her like a wave, making her tremble as she cries out in pleasure.

Luca gets up getting a warm cloth cleaning her breasts while I bring her down from the orgasmic high.

Once she relaxes, I kiss a path up her body until I reach those full, plump lips. I claim them, making sure she can feel my emotions. When I pull back, she's breathless, staring into my eyes. I cup her face before speaking. "You're ours."

Sam buries her fingers in my hair, never breaking eye contact. "And you're mine." I smile, knowing tonight is the first night of many.

We settle in. Luca wrapping his arm around her waist, his leg draped over hers. "Ours," he echoes, burying his face in her neck.

"Yes," Sam replies, placing a hand over Luca and one over me.

"Get some sleep, mia regina," I say, molding my larger frame tight against hers. She seems so small between us.

Her eyes flutter closed, exhaustion finally overtaking her. I squeeze my eyes closed, willing my shaft to go down, chanting in my head that the first time I come, it will be deep inside her. Luca may be content by marking her skin, but I need to claim her body. Every part of her. Once I finally sink into her tight little body, it will know who owns it.

She'll be here by our side tomorrow and every night after. She's ours now, and we'll never let her go.

Chapter 10

Sam

I slowly wake up, opening my eyes and realizing there are two hard bodies pressed up against me. The morning sun is bright, filtering through the windows, and I squint. As I tilt my head back, I see that my upper body's draped across Marco's chest. Luca presses his hard shaft into my back, and our legs are tangled together.

Memories of last night flood my mind and I smile. They were both so focused on me it was almost overwhelming, but I'm not complaining. It was the most amazing night of my life. I lift my head and kiss Marco's chest and slide Luca's hand from around me before climbing out of bed.

Marco throws his arm over his eyes and I pause mid step. "Come back to bed." His deep baritone voice is sexy in the morning.

"I need the bathroom, then food," I say before grabbing some clothes from my suitcase and entering the ensuite. Turning the shower on, I undress, then quickly wash and shampoo my hair. Once I'm done, I dry off before finishing my morning routine. Putting my long hair up in a messy ponytail out of my face.

After picking up my clothes that need laundered, I exit the bathroom to see my gorgeous men dressed and waiting for me. I swallow hard so I don't drool at the sight. These two in suits should be a sin. Does their tailor purposefully design them to make their muscles more pronounced?

Their eyes slowly look me up and down, appraising me, but I clear my throat before placing my dirty clothes on top of my suitcase. I'll wash them later. Clearing my throat, I walk out of the bedroom to search for Jules. I find her sitting at the bar in the kitchen, smiling mischievously. I throw her a wink before getting a glass from the cabinet and pouring some juice.

Jules stares at me for a moment before leaning forward on the bar. "So?"

"So, nothing. I slept amazing," I say with a grin and she huffs at me, frustrated.

Marco and Luca come in, each of them kissing me on the cheek. Luca cups my face in his hands and stares into my eyes with such intensity I have to press my thighs together. "We have to work for a while. Stay here so we know you're safe."

I nod. One day, in a luxurious penthouse won't kill me. But I'll call Uncle Fred later to check on things, just to be sure.

When Luca releases me, Marco takes my chin between his fingers, tilting my head back to look up at him. "We'll be back in a few hours. Meanwhile, I'll have breakfast delivered."

That has my stomach growling, making them both chuckle. I shrug, but I can feel the heat rising to my cheeks. "I've got a healthy appetite." My voice is playful, trying to ease my embarrassment.

Thirty minutes after they left, food arrived. Jules and I sat in the dining room eating and the silence is deafening. "I'm going to go stir-crazy here."

Jules snickered at me as she began cleaning up. "Let's find some cards or something to play while we talk." I agree, before helping her clean up our mess.

After finally finding a deck of cards in a side table drawer, we began playing poker. I dealt her three cards, replacing her throw-a-ways, and she grinned. "So you're really not going to give me any details about last night?"

I take two replacement cards for myself before raising my eyes to meet hers. "Nope."

"Fine." She leans back in her chair and huffs. "How long do you think we'll be staying here?"

I lay my cards down and think of an answer. There isn't one. "It depends. But at least you don't have to worry about Steve anymore."

Jules scrunches her nose up in disgust before laying her cards down. "Flush."

"Shit," I say, flipping mine over, revealing three of a kind. She always beats me at cards.

Sliding my phone from my back pocket, I see it's noon. I scroll to find Uncle Fred's number and hit dial. The wondering if he's heard or seen anything, is eating at me.

LUST AND BLOOD

Jules leans forward, watching me closely, so I hit speaker and lay my phone on the table. This whole situation affects her too. "Hey, Sam." Uncle Fred's voice sounds tired, like he hasn't slept.

"Hey, Uncle Fred, everything ok?" I know he can hear the concern in my voice.

He sighs before answering, making my eyebrows furrow. "Ya, just a long night."

"What happened?" I ask, biting my lip.

"Nothing at the house. It's all quiet there and at Jules, thankfully. I just couldn't sleep." I know he's worried, but there's something else he's not saying.

"Tell her or I will." I hear Roger's voice in the background, then rustling like Uncle Fred covers the phone. Oh, hell no. He's not keeping secrets from me.

"Tell me now." He knows I'm like a dog with a bone and I won't let this go. If something happened, he needs to spill it.

He growls, and I wait for him to explain. "Crawley came by, and we had words."

"More than words," Rogers says loud enough that I hear through the phone.

Crawley, I know that name. Shit, that's the name of that developer. I fist my hands, trying to control my anger. "Tell me everything."

"The pushy little prick wasn't taking no for an answer. Offered a million for the property this time, and I told him to shove it up his ass before leaving." Uncle Fred goes quiet, and I know there's more.

"And?" I drag out the word, coaching him to continue.

"And before walking out, the little shit said it would be a shame if something happened to the place. So I decked his ass good." Roger's laughter in the background does nothing to calm me. Crawley made a threat. A threat not only to our livelihood but a place I grew up in and love as much as Uncle Fred.

"Fucker," I say under my breath, but Jules and Uncle Fred both catch it. Jules is covering her mouth, and I see the concern in her eyes. Crawley has gone too far. "What do you want to do?"

I have to know how Uncle Fred wants to handle this. Although he made me an equal partner on my 21st birthday, in the business with him and Roger, it's Uncle Fred who makes the actual decisions, and I respect him enough to follow his lead.

I hear him opening the fridge then closing it, making me wonder if it's water he's getting or a beer under the circumstances. "I'm going to stay here tonight since you're away just to be safe. He may try something."

I lean back in my chair, feeling a knot form in my stomach. "I'm staying too," Roger says, making me feel a little better. Not that I mind them in my apartment, but the thought I'm not there for him after all he's done for me makes the knot tighten a little more.

"Do you want me to come back?" He knows I will in a heartbeat, even though I hate the thought of doing it after the night I had with Marco and Luca.

"No," Uncle Fred says without hesitation. "You girls stay there until the dust settles. We've got things handled."

"Ok." I give him the answer he wants, but it doesn't ease my anxiety any.

Jules and I continue to play cards for the next hour, laughing and talking until she gets a curious expression while shuffling the cards. "Are you serious about them?"

Her question takes me a little off guard, but Jules and I have always talked about everything. "Yes, even though it scares the shit out of me."

Jules laughs, then covers her mouth. "I'm sorry, it's not funny. But the idea of something scaring you is funny." She sits straight, lays the cards down, and then takes my hand. "What are you afraid of?"

I groan and lean my head back against the chair, staring at the ceiling. "Everything. Something happening to them. Them hurting me." I admit the truth, rolling my head to the side, staring at her.

Jules looks sad and squeezes my hand. "You're afraid of what we all are, that they'll break your heart."

"Yes," I whisper. "I'm not from their world, Jules. The only thing we have in common is when shit goes down, we handle it hardcore." I'm unsure where the words come from, but they're true. Maybe it's my subconscious talking to her, I think as I feel tears filling my eyes.

Jules looks as if she's going to cry with me until her eyes shift, looking past me. I sit up and turn, seeing Marco and Luca standing at the edge of the dining room. When did they get here? Jules stands and excuses herself.

As soon as she is past them, Marco and Luca charge toward me with determined steps. Marco jerks me from my chair, slamming me against the wall

LUST AND BLOOD

so hard the air leaves my lungs. I grip the lapels of his suit, and he fists my hair, forcing me to look up at him. "I better never hear you say you're not part of our world again. You. Are. Our. Fucking. World." His words hit me hard, and my stomach filled with butterflies. Marco slams his mouth on mine in a demanding kiss. He wastes no time pushing his tongue past my lips, plunging deep and tasting every inch of my mouth. A gasp escapes when he pulls my hair tighter, causing my scalp to burn, and he presses his body into mine, grinding his hard shaft into me.

I respond, instantly pushing my breasts into him and trying to give my hard nipples some attention. I'm so turned on, and I can feel my panties being soaked. Marco pulls back, leaning his forehead on mine. "Don't you ever forget that."

When he steps away, Luca immediately picks me up, and I wrap my legs around him, holding onto his shoulders for support. I could barely hold the squeal in. "I thought we made it clear last night that you belong to us."

Meeting his gaze, I nod in response, but his hard look says he's not satisfied with that. Luca's hand goes around my throat, squeezing enough he has my full attention. "Mine." His lips meet mine in a slow, deliberate kiss. It's consuming and claiming.

I thread my fingers into his hair and tug as I grind my needy, aching core down into him. The growl that rumbles from his chest tells me he feels the same want that I do. I don't want to wait any longer. My body craves them, and now my head and heart are on the same page. I'll trust them both with all of me.

Marco comes up behind me and grips my ass with both hands. "Let's move this to the bedroom, brother. She deserves a bed the first time we take her." My greedy core spasms at the thought of having them.

Chapter 11

Sam

Marco takes off toward our bedroom, and Luca carries me behind him, devouring my mouth the entire way. He growls into my mouth each time I grind myself down into him, arousing me even more. When Luca stops walking, I hear the door shut and lock. I open my eyes as I pull away from the toe-curling kiss.

Marco presses against my spine, fisting my hair as he pulls my head back. "I hope you're ready for us, Mia Regina, because we've waited too long to claim you as ours." I swallow hard but nod because hell, yes, I'm more than ready.

Luca grazes his teeth over my ear, making tingles ripple down my spine before setting me on my feet. His eyes are full of love but also a promise this will be a night I'll never forget. I feel like prey as his gaze travels lower, taking me in before adjusting himself.

Marco turns me, facing him, and grips my chin, tilting my head up. "We're forever mia regina, no going back." Those words have both my heart and body melting. I'm theirs, and they're mine. Every part of me knows it. The sound of clothing being removed behind me has butterflies erupting in my stomach. Luca's undressing.

Marco lifts me into his muscular arms, laying me on the bed. Once he has my pants and panties off, I lift to remove my shirt for them. Marco stands straight, slowly removing his clothes and my nipples tighten so hard they're aching.

When Luca steps closer, my eyes go to his, seeing the feral look in them. It's so raw and full of need that my breath hitches. He starts at my feet and trails his palms up to my knees before pushing them apart. I'm open and exposed to them both. All the embarrassment I thought I'd feel my first time is nowhere to be seen. The need to be touched and filled by them is so powerful it's consuming me.

"Exquisite mia regina," Luca says, staring at my core. "I'm going to eat your delicious pussy until you scream my name. And once I'm satisfied, we'll claim what's ours." When his eyes climb up my body, meeting mine, I see the carnal need inside him. It matches mine. Luca kneels, licking from my opening to my clit, sucking hard. I throw my head back and moan out at the pleasure shooting through me. It's as if lightning has struck me.

He grips my legs tight, throwing them over his shoulders before eating me like a starving man. Pure ecstasy rushes through me, and I have trouble catching my breath. My instincts kick in and I fist two handfuls of his hair, holding on tight. Luca inserts a finger and begins stroking over a spot that has my legs shaking. When he moves faster, my ass shoots off the bed, making him growl into me.

"Luca," I moan loudly, and he increases his speed. My core tightens on his finger as my legs shake uncontrollably.

A pinch to my nipples has my eyes shooting open to see Marco now kneeling on the bed next to me. When he does it again, my orgasm rips through me like a firestorm and I scream. It's only muffled when Marco slams his mouth onto mine. He pulls back when I come down from the high. "Seeing you come apart is the most erotic thing I've seen."

Luca stands, his face glistening with my wetness, with a broad grin. When he licks his lips, tasting me on them, arousal floods me again. My eyes flick down, seeing him fisting his enormous dick. He moves to the chair in the corner, sitting with his eyes boring into mine. "Soon mia regina."

Marco slides me up the bed onto a pillow before kissing up my legs, my stomach, to finally meeting my eyes. His body is hovering over mine when he uses his legs to push mine apart. My entire body is vibrating with anticipation and he can see it. "No going back, and never doubt our commitment to you," he says before gently kissing my lips. It's slow and sensual, but holds so much promise.

Marco takes his throbbing cock and runs the mushroom head through my folds, up to my sensitive clit. When he notches it at my entrance, his eyes lock onto mine before pushing forward. Once the head is in, I feel a burn I've never known before and Marco claims my lips, swallowing my whimper.

LUST AND BLOOD

He fills me slowly, stretching me to fit his thickness, and I feel his hand move to massage my clit between us. All the sensations flooding my body are overwhelming. Pleasure, pain, it's such exquisite torture and I love it.

Luca's growl coming from the corner of the room has me looking in his direction, briefly seeing him stroking his length and watching us. Marco thrusts forward. Bottoming out against my womb has me sucking in a harsh breath as tears prick my eyes. "All of me, mia regina. You will have all of me, as I will have all of you." His eyes are so intense, staring at me. I feel like our souls are just as connected as our bodies.

Pleasure and pain mix, taking my breath away. I wrap my legs around his waist while running my nails down his back. "All of us," I say, staring into his eyes.

"You're mine." It's almost a growl, and he rotates his hips, grinding deep. "Dig those heels into my back, mia regina, and hold on."

I sink my teeth into his shoulder and dig my nails into his back as he pulls back, then thrusts deep. Marco grunts when my walls clamp down on him, making him thicken more inside me. Pleasure is coursing through me, and I lift my hips, meeting his thrusts. The pain has faded and I embrace the pleasure.

His strokes are hard and determined as he claims me, making the headboard slam into the wall. Our eyes remain locked and our bodies move as one. My orgasm is building fast with him hitting that perfect spot deep inside with every stroke and he can see it in my expression. "Fuck Sam," he says as I tighten on him, unable to control what's happening to my body. I embrace it.

Like a tree splitting apart from a lightning strike, I explode around him, screaming out. "Marco." I feel his whole body go rigid before slamming himself balls deep. "Fuck." That one word echoes off the walls as he holds me tight until our bodies come down from our high. Once the jerking and twitching fades, Marco leans down, kissing me softly.

I bury my fingers in his hair, raking my nails over his scalp while our tongues taste each other. At this moment, with our bodies joined, I feel so loved. The air is thick with it. He pulls back, kissing my forehead before rolling to the side.

Luca approaches the bed, kissing up my body, spreading my legs wide as he does. Once he reaches my face, he sits up on his knees, jerking me up onto his lap, straddling him. My arms immediately wrap around him for support. "Mia

Regina, sit on your throne and take your rightful place." His words slam into me. Not that he's asking me to ride him, but now I know what Mia Regina is after all the times they've said it. My queen. They are calling me their queen.

I raise myself, and he positions the head of his dick at my entrance. Never taking my eyes off Luca's intense gaze, I slowly sink down onto him, feeling the stretch and burn coming back in full force. "This is the only time you'll have control in the bedroom. Enjoy it."

I feel his words down to my bones. These are dominant men who demand control in every aspect of their lives. I can give them that in the bedroom. A deep hidden part of me craves it. Once he's filled me and I'm stretched wide for him, I meet his stare with a determined one. "Take it." Daring him to do whatever he desires with me. A flash of heat sparks in his eyes before he snarls. Luca slams me down onto the bed and hooks his arms behind my knees, opening me wide. "Be careful what you wish for mia regina." I'm open and vulnerable in this position, and he slams into me, shooting my body up the bed. "Don't run from what you asked for," he says with a smirk before jerking my body back to him.

The bolt of pleasure that ripped through me only fuels me more. I want everything he has to give me, even if it means I can't walk for days. "So tight," he groans, thrusting into me. He's claiming me like a feral animal, and I love it.

Marco pinches my nipples, and I grab his hair roughly, pulling him down. Nothing else matters except the three of us when he takes my lips with his. The entire world fades away.

Luca's pace becomes erratic. He's animalistic, slamming into me in long, demanding thrusts, making me continuously moan. My legs are trembling, and he lowers himself, encasing me in his muscular hold. His biceps flexing against my thighs in time with his movements.

Suddenly, my stomach tightens and I clamp down hard on Lucas. His name leaves me in a scream. "Luca."

When I throw my head back at the intensity of what's happening, he bites my neck. His relentless pace carries me through the endless waves of pleasure coursing through me. He swells even more inside me, hitting my cervix with each thrust forward until he holds himself against it.

Luca's body shakes as he pulses inside me, filling me up. "Mine." It's one word I'll never tire of hearing. After he finishes emptying inside me, he collapses

LUST AND BLOOD

onto my chest. I feel my hair being brushed aside and turn to Marco, who is looking down at me with so much love. He bends, kissing along my jaw to my mouth.

Luca raises and rolls to my side, pulling me tight against him. I lay my head on his chest as Marco pulls the sheet up, covering us all. I feel complete with Marco pressed against my back and Luca to my front, both keeping me in a tight embrace.

My body would be happy if I never had to move again, but I know it's inevitable. We haven't eaten dinner yet, and I'm worried about Uncle Fred and the little shit that threatened him.

Marco tightens his arm around my waist before I hear his rough voice. "I can almost hear your thoughts you're thinking so hard. What is it, Sam?"

I sigh because I didn't want to ruin our moment. But I won't hide things from them. Luca kisses the top of my head, and I know they're both waiting. I trace slow circles on Luca and tell them everything from earlier today and my concerns.

To my surprise, Marco and Luca agree we should stop by the garage after eating dinner. "Seeing Uncle Fred while eating out is the second best way to end the night," I say, grinning.

Marco pulls me, turning me on my back before hovering, his face just inches from mine. "And what would be the first?" He asks with a glint in his eyes.

"Not to leave the bed until morning," I reply with a grin. Luca's deep chuckle from beside me makes me laugh.

Chapter 12

Luca

During dinner at Romano's, Sam sits between us. Marco and I can't keep our hands off of her now. Each of us palming a thigh beneath the table. After claiming her, the need to have her near and touch her is more intense.

The moment I saw her at the club, she drew me in. A perfect woman that I had given up hope of finding. Everything about her makes me crave more. To know her likes and dislikes as well as how she thinks. I look past her over to Marco, seeing the same possessiveness I feel. We are in love with her. A warmth settles in my chest and I reach up, rubbing it.

As she and Jules talk about the garage, my gaze moves to Marco. I want her to carry our last name, hell our babies, everything. When he looks back at me, his jaw ticks. We've always been close and had a connection. Often in meetings, reading each other's thoughts without speaking a word. I watch him study my face, then lean back in his chair. When he gives me a nod, I know we're on the same page. We want everything now to figure out the how.

I relax back in my seat, thoughts swirling in my head. First, we need to convince Sam to become legally ours, and then we'll find a way.

I'm brought out of my thoughts when Lou walks into our private dining room, followed by the waiter. "What can I get you, sir?" the waiter asks Lou as he sits beside Jules.

"Whiskey, double," Lou says, never taking his eyes off of Jules. When her face flushes, I know she is as attracted to him as he is to her. Wouldn't it be something if things worked out between them? I feel Sam's hand running up my thigh and look down. She's doing the same to Marco and I groan low.

This woman is going to be the death of me, is my only thought as she stops just short of my crotch and squeezes my thigh. She slyly side-eyes me and I lean down, brushing my lips over her ear. "Tease me, mia regina, and you'll pay later."

Sam sucks in a breath and I don't miss the shiver that runs through her. Good, because I can't wait to show her what genuine pleasure is. We were gentle by our standards with her tonight. I sit back and smirk at her while Marco whispers something in her other ear, causing her to squeeze her legs together. I chuckle darkly before taking a drink.

Lou's whiskey arrives, and he takes a long drink before curiosity gets the better of him. "What's your plan for tonight?" he asks, looking around the table.

I lean forward and fill him in on the shit that's happened at the garage. Lou's face goes hard, and he looks at Jules. "I'm coming. If there's an issue, we'll handle it." Oh, doesn't he know how independent these women are?

I smirk and watch as Jules sits straighter and jets her chin out. "Handle it?" Oh damn, she's pissed. Sam leans into me, laughing as we watch Jules' face go red. "I don't need a daddy to handle things for me. We. Can. Handle. Things. Ourselves. Just. Fine."

Lou sits his drink down and cups the back of her head. I watch with amusement as he puts his face right in hers while holding her in place. "Call me that again." Jules looks confused for a moment until she realizes what he's saying.

Her face goes beat red, then she sucks in a breath. "You..."

She doesn't get to finish because he gets closer, so their noses are almost touching. "Go on, say it," Lou says, daring her. Jules shakes her head no, and he scoops her up, walking out of the room with determined strides. We all laugh, watching him storm out. That girl doesn't know what she's started with him.

Sam tilts her head back, looking up at me. "If he hurts her, I'll cut his balls off." I nod, knowing she would. But Lou is a good man. I've never seen him act this way with a woman.

"He'll treat her right," Marco says, expressing my thoughts.

Sam pulls her phone out, checking the time. "We should go. It's after 8."

I take her hand, kissing the back while Marco stands buttoning his jacket. We need to ease her mind. Hell, I'd do anything for her. We need to look into this Crawley guy and his company. Anyone fucking with our woman's family is fucking with us.

LUST AND BLOOD

When we reach the top of the stairs, I see Lou and Jules exiting the bathroom, hand in hand. She has swollen lips and messy hair. Well, I guess they sorted things out. We all go down getting into the SUV's heading to the garage.

As we pulling into the parking lot at Gearheads, it's so quiet I can hear the gravel crunching under the tires. Opening my door so I can help Sam out, the smell of motor oil and gasoline permeates the air. I close my door then open Sam's, taking her hand as Lou and Jules park beside us.

The women smile at each other while Marco takes Sam's other hand. Before we can take a step toward the building, the world explodes around us. We feel the deafening blast and the explosion lifts our bodies. We're being thrown back by the shockwaves. The garage erupts into a blinding flash and flames are everywhere. Time seems to slow and shards of glass and twisted metal hurtle through the air with us.

I hit the ground hard, pain exploding in my shoulder as I skid across the rough pavement. All sound is gone except the ringing in my ears drowning everything out. Once I'm able to suck in a painful breath, the smell of smoke and burning rubber fills my senses. Sam, I need to get to Sam.

Marco scrambles past me and my eyes follow before my body moves. He's gripping Sam's shoulders as she lays a few feet away from me. I'm instantly on my hands and knees, crawling to her other side. Marco's lips are moving, but I can't hear the words and Sam's look of confusion tells me she can't either.

After we assess her for injuries, only seeing a few minor cuts on her face from flying glass, we pull her to her feet. I keep her hand in mine as we all scan the surrounding devastation. What used to be the garage is now a smoldering pile of rubble and twisted metal. Flames are high, making the heat radiating from it impossible to get closer.

My chest constricts when I spot Uncle Fred's truck parked off to the side. The horrible reality sinking in. He and Roger were inside.

Sam releases our hands and slams both fists into her chest, screaming. "Uncle Fred! No!" Her pain-filled scream breaks through the ringing in my ears. It's raw and pain rips through my chest seeing her agony. Her last living blood relative is gone. Not just gone, but basically dying the same way her parents did.

When her knees buckle, I'm quick to grab her waist, supporting her Marco taking her other side. Seeing he has her weight supported, I bend, scooping her up into my arms. Sam curls into my chest, screaming. There are no recognizable words formed, just gut-wrenching pain leaving her.

Marco steps to her back, stroking her hair gently as Jules and Lou come to our sides. I honestly had forgotten about them.

My eyes lock onto Marco's and pure rage rises in me. "He's dead. Everyone involved is dead. We burn them and everything they care about to the ground."

I grind my teeth together at his words. It won't be enough for what they've done, but it's a start. "Yes." It's the only word I'm able to spit out under the circumstances. First, we take care of our woman. She will always come first.

I walk to the SUV and Marco opens the door. Sam grips my shirt tighter, and I know I can't put her down. "I'm only sitting with you, mia regina, not letting you go."

She buries her head in my neck and I watch Marco's jaw flex. He has the same war building inside as I do. This Crawley doesn't know the level of war and destruction we are about to unleash on him, but we'll educate him soon enough.

Chapter 13

Marco

    I slide the key into the ignition, gritting my teeth. The need to hold Sam and comfort her is the only thing keeping my urge to destroy everything that has ever hurt her at bay. The tires squeal as I pull out of the parking lot, followed closely by Lou.

    I know he must be upset that Jules is riding with us, but she refused to leave Sam's side. A quick glance in the rear-view mirror calms me as I see Jules stroking Sam's hair as tears roll down her cheeks.

    With my eyes back on the road, I attempt to gather my thoughts. I understand her uncle was her last living blood relative, but her scream was bloodcurdling, and the pain she expressed was beyond anything I've seen between a niece and uncle. Was it the death of her parents that brought them so close, or did something else happen? Maybe one day she'll tell me.

    One thing's certain. This Crawley and everything he has will pay with blood for his actions. I will make it especially painful before ending him. My eyes flick back to the mirror as we approach the penthouse. Sam's eyes are closed, letting me know she's passed out from exhaustion. When Luca kisses her forehead, inhaling her scent, I grip the steering wheel with such force it cracks.

    "Easy, brother. You'll have the rest of the night to hold her." Luca's low voice soothes my need to have her close.

    Once I park, I'm immediately out of the vehicle, opening the door for Luca. We need to get our woman upstairs. Sam opens her eyes as Luca stands, cradling her to his chest. The look in her eyes has my chest cracking open. She looks like she's shattered and drained of that fighting spirit I love. Resolve washes over me. She'll get it back when we get our retribution.

We enter the building and go straight for our private elevator. I am beside Luca and Sam while Lou hovers over Jules. However, he doesn't get off on his floor but comes to ours escorting Jules to her room while we take care of Sam.

Luca places Sam in the center of the bed after I pull the covers back. We don't bother undressing her, only removing her shoes. I pull the sheet up, but she doesn't move except to curl further into the pillows. I raise my head, looking at Luca, and without a word, I gesture to the door. We need to talk while she rests.

Lou meets us in the living room, his expression tense as we all sit. "Boss, I've got a team ready to roll. We'll dig into Crawley's life like he's an open book. His routines, his home, his business dealings. Everything."

My fingers drum against the armrest as I nod. Visions of torturing the man who caused Sam's pain playing on repeat in my head. "Good. Get everything you can. We're going to tear him apart." Just as Luca was about to speak, Sam entered. By her expression, she's heard everything.

"Like hell you're doing this without me," she says, coming closer.

Before she can protest, Luca and I guide her to the couch, wrapping her in our arms. Jules comes in, her features etched with concern, and sits across from us.

"How are you holding up, Sam?" It's obvious she's been crying. Making it clear she was close with Fred and Roger as well.

Sam's response is vulnerable, making my chest tighten. "The pain morphed into anger. I want vengeance." The hardness of her words doesn't match her voice. But after seeing her deal with Steve, I won't doubt what she's capable of.

I hold her tighter, letting her words ignite something primal within me. "Tell us, Sam. What brought you and Uncle Fred so close?" The question comes out without conscious thought, which isn't like me. I always choose my words carefully.

She takes a deep breath before staring off like she's remembering. "It all started the night my parents died."

Sam's voice trembles as she recounts the horrors of that night. The screams, the smell of smoke, the helplessness of being carried away from her burning home. "I fought him every step of the way," she continues, her eyes distant as she relives the memories. "Hitting, scratching him, and screaming." A tear falls, and she wipes at her cheek, choking back a sob.

LUST AND BLOOD

"My teenage years were worse. Some things I said and did blaming him..." She stops, shaking her head like she wishes she could take it all back. "But Uncle Fred never gave up on me. He showed me that love and time can heal almost anything."

Sam stops, then takes my hand in hers and Luca's in the other. I watch, waiting while she looks between us, trying to find the words she's searching for. "For years, I believed that night was the worst thing I'd experience. I was wrong. Tonight has been the darkest moment of my life, but you're everything I need."

Fucking hell, this woman will be the death of me. I grab her, smashing my lips on hers. I put everything I have into it. My love, my devotion, even the anger I've been pushing down deep. She gets it all and clings to me as I give it to her. When I pull back, she's dazed and out of breath as Luca pulls her onto his lap.

He cups her face, gently stroking her jawline. "I'll always be what you need, mia regina. Anything." His lips brush over hers, revealing a soft side to him I didn't know existed. Sam brings out the best in both of us. Anyone who threatens that will wish they crossed the devil himself instead by the time I get through with them.

When Luca releases her face and pulls back, Sam turns to Jules with a sad smile. "I meant you too, in that you know. Forever, remember?"

"Forever," Jules says, wiping her tears.

The hours go by slowly as we discuss arrangements for Roger and Uncle Fred, knowing the condition they will be in for burial. "I want them buried as soon as possible. Uncle Fred hated funerals and goodbyes."

"Ok, we'll arrange everything with the funeral home." I take her hand, squeezing it as her phone rings in the other room. I glance at Luca, knowing it's probably the police calling to notify Sam of what happened. He nods at me before going to take care of it. Sam has enough to deal with.

Finally, by sunrise, we're all too exhausted to function, so we go to bed for some much-needed sleep. I know tomorrow will be difficult and we'll have a lot of plans to make after Lou gets the information we need.

We strip Sam getting her into bed before Luca and I do the same, flanking each side of her. "Thank you," Sam says. Her voice is barely a whisper. I pull her tighter against me and kiss the top of her head. "Always, mia regina."

Luca buries his face in her neck, inhaling deeply. "Forever."

Chapter 14

Sam

Two days later, we stand in the cemetery. The scent of rain and freshly turned earth is thick in the air. It makes sense that even the heavens are crying at the death of two wonderful men. The cold hard truth that they're gone is like a vice squeezing my chest.

I'm filled with pain, and only a few words come to mind, so they're all I say. "I love you. Goodbye." Everything seems like a blur. The only thing grounding me is the feel of Marco's hand gripping mine, Luca's arms around me from behind like a solid wall at my back. Jules grips my other hand. Her face is pink from crying, but she remains silent.

I stare at the roses we each laid on Uncle Fred and Roger's graves, knowing they will fade and die within days. Something deep inside me vows that we'll end Crawley before that happens. We turn away as the slow mist of rain hits my face. It does nothing to cool the hot vengeance racking me. Marco, Luca, and Lou guide us back to the SUVs. Their hands never leave my skin, keeping me grounded.

When we all arrive at the penthouse, the men lead Jules and me into their office. The air seems even more tense, making me wonder what's going on. Marco sits behind his large mahogany desk, pulling me onto his lap while Luca retrieves a file from a wall safe.

Luca hands it to me, and Marco tightens his hold around my waist. I open it and see a picture of an older, thin man with a smug face staring back at me. I study it for a moment before flipping through the pages and reading.

The more I read, the more my eyes become blurry from the rising tears. Not from sadness, but from pure rage. The greed and ruthlessness of this horrible man is beyond my imagination. Crawley Development has been buying up all the surrounding property of Gearheads by any means necessary. Many business owners who refused him were hospitalized or, worse. It's like looking at puzzle pieces and they fall into place before your eyes.

Our land is the last piece he needs for a major high-rise condo community that, by the plans I'm looking at, will make the Southside the new place to be. We were the final holdout, unknowingly putting us in his crosshairs. He made a mistake, though. I am an equal owner. He didn't get us all. "Bastard!" I slam the file closed and meet Luca's gaze.

His eyes are dark and deadly, sharing my anger. "We take him out." Luca's voice is like steel.

Marco turns me, facing him, and holds my face in his large, callused hands. "We destroy everything he's built."

I nod, my mind racing with all the pain that Crawley deserves before he dies. Then I remember something. "Uncle Fred's basement," I say, looking around the room. "He kept weapons down there. It's only fitting we use them to end Crawley."

For the first time in days, Jules burst out laughing but tries to cover it with her hands. I smile, but it's not pleasant. It's evil, as I envision the man in the folder bleeding out slowly.

Lou's eyes light up with a dangerous glint. "Let's get them."

Luca takes my hand, pulling me from Marco's lap. We all return to the SUVs, and my body hums with anticipation. At Uncle Fred's, I lead them down to the basement. I take my time as memories of growing up here flash through my mind. I push them away for now as I open the gun cabinets and drawers, revealing weapons and ammunition. "Shit," Marco says, taking everything in.

Uncle Fred was a gun enthusiast. Luca and Lou load up arms full of guns, ammo, and gear into vehicles while Marco holds me close. Jules silently stays at my side, looking around the basement where we used to come to share our deepest secrets.

We all help with the last load of weapons. I close my eyes at the SUV's back door to take a deep breath. The scent of gun oil and dust on my clothes and hands seems to give me a strange comfort. When I open them again, Marco and Luca are standing so close it startles me for a minute.

They pull me into a hard embrace between them before Marco brushes his lips against my ear. "We've got this, Sam. Crawley won't know what hit him."

LUST AND BLOOD

I nod and bury my face in his chest. Luca presses further into me and I feel his warm breath against my cheek. "We'll make him pay in blood for everything." Something lets loose inside me. I know taking Crawley out won't bring them back, but I deserve retribution and he won't be able to hurt anyone else. That will be enough.

Back at the penthouse, we lay everything out in a weapons room I hadn't noticed before. The Rizzo's arsenal is massive compared to Uncle Fred's collection. Marco, Luca, and Lou go over a plan using city maps. I step closer to listen and watch with Jules right at my side. They detail every step of an elaborate plan to blow his building up using an explosive expert in the Rizzo family while we take Crawley out at his residence.

Jules turns to me, her eyes filled with worry. "Are you ok?" I know she isn't used to being around this type of thing. Hell, neither am I. But this will be my life now. My life with my men, I knew that the moment I gave them my heart.

Jules gives me a soft smile and nods. "I'm in," she says. I'm shocked she wants to be involved, but I shouldn't be. She's always been stronger than she realizes.

With a mischievous grin, I lead her to the table of guns we brought from Uncle Fred's. I pick up a 9mm. I remember her shooting when we were teenagers. He taught us to respect guns and to shoot for protection.

Jules takes it with a sad smile before picking up a full clip. She locks it into place, chambers a round then ensures the safety is on. When her eyes raise to mine, I give her a nod of appreciation that she remembers everything we learned. I don't miss the look of surprise on Lou's face at watching her handle a gun.

I shake my head, pick up a matching 9mm, and do the same. Locked, loaded, and ready for action, I stuff it into my waistband before turning to my men. I'll get my favorite out of my glove compartment later. The one in my waist was Uncle Fred's. It will be the one that ends Crawley.

After hours of going over the plans, we all sit around the dining room table with takeout. Marco and Luca each take one of my hands. Marco gets a hard look, and I tilt my head, studying his face. "We do this in two teams. No one veers from the plan." When I nod in understanding, he looks around the table as if making sure everyone follows his order.

MEL PATE

We finish eating while going over the plan one last time, leaving no room for error. Jules will go with Lou and his team to watch the charges being set on his building before they meet us at Crawley's estate. Marco, Luca, and I will be at the edge of his property, watching his mansion.

Once the building's blown, he will receive word and leave to check it out. He won't be able to resist seeing it for himself. As soon as he's on the road off the property, we attack, trapping him in the vehicle. Lou and his crew coming up from behind, leaving no escape route. Us attacking from the front. I, of course, demand to be the one putting a bullet in his head. Crawley won't know what's happening until it's too late.

Jules goes to her room to get some sleep and Lou leaves to assemble the team. We strike at 4 a.m. I take both Marco's and Luca's hands, leading them to our room. We need rest.

Chapter 15

Luca

The incessant ringing of Marco's phone jolts me awake. I pry my eyes open as he answers it in a terse voice. Sam stirs slightly on my chest and I hold her tighter while listening to Marco's side of the conversation. It's obviously Lou; he's talking, too. Then I hear Crawley's name and mention of the development company. I hold back the snarl at the mere mention of him and listen closer.

"Fine, take Crawley and his men to the warehouse at the docks. We'll be there in an hour. He better be breathing when we arrive." Marco ends the call and turns towards me with an annoyed expression.

"Tell me, brother." My rough voice wakes Sam, pissing me off. She needs rest.

Sam rubs her face before looking at us. "What's going on?"

Marco stands, pulling his boxers on before saying a word. "Change of plans. Crawley and three men worked late. So he isn't at his estate. They're leaving the development company now. Our men are grabbing them and taking them to the warehouse. Get ready baby."

Sam throws the covers off both of us, but I grab her before she jumps out of bed, kissing her. "Take your time. He'll be there when we arrive." She nods, taking a deep breath, but I see that fire blazing in her eyes. It's sexy as hell when she's ready to hurt someone. My dick twitches and I reach down, squeezing it. I'm a twisted fuck and I own that shit.

Without wasting time, I get dressed and check my weapon before tucking it into my waist. Sam exits the bathroom, and Marco enters, determined to get down to the warehouse. I walk to her as she retrieves her Uncle Fred's 9mm and runs her fingers over the barrel.

When she lifts her head, meeting my eyes, I see the fierce woman on the outside, but there's no hiding the pain reeling in her eyes. Crawley will get both from her. I have no doubt. She puts the gun at her back and I take her hand in mine, offering both my strength and support should she need it tonight.

The ride to the warehouse is quiet, and the tension is palpable. Sam sits in the passenger seat with me driving and Marco took the back. All our gazes fixed on the road ahead. I pull up to the side entrance, the scent of water and fish mixing in the cool night air.

Marco helps Sam out of the SUV, keeping her hand in his while I take her other. We will do this as a family. This one time, she'll take the lead. After everything Sam's been through, she deserves vengeance.

Entering, our footsteps against the cold, hard concrete in the large open space. Crawley's tied to a chair in the center, his hands and feet bound to the arms and legs. Someone clearly beat him. Blood is trickling from his nose and mouth, and his right eye's swollen shut. I give an appreciative nod to Lou and our men before they turn, walking to the far side of the warehouse.

Looking down at our Mia Regina, I see her beautiful face contorted in fury and pain. Her jaw's set and there is a promise of pain in her eyes. Crawley deserves every ounce of pain she's about to inflict. And if she can't, Marco and I will do it for her before ending him.

Sam pulls her eyes off of Crawley, taking in the warehouse. The table we keep various instruments of torture on catches her eye. She walks to it as if in a daze, letting her fingertips graze over each item. Marco and I move in unison, staying at her side. She isn't in this alone. She'll face nothing on her own again.

Her hand hovers over a favorite of mine. It's a fillet knife. The curved thin blade makes it an excellent tool. "That's a fish fillet knife," I say, stepping closer to her and placing my hand on the small of her back. "Used on the docks. It makes precise, clean cuts. There's nothing better except maybe a scalpel."

Sam nods, almost in a trance, before laying it down. Instead, she picks up a drill. The sight of it in her small hands when she pulls the trigger, making it hum to life, is chilling. Marco and I stay two steps behind her as she approaches Crawley and his men, letting her take the lead.

Crawley's eyes widen in terror when she stops in front of him, pulling the trigger again. Sam presses it to his forearm strapped to the arm of the chair, drilling through flesh and what sounded like bone. The scream that rips from his throat is raw as his eyes roll back in his head.

LUST AND BLOOD

Sam pulls it back away from him, staring down into his face with disgust and rage. "Tell me about the people you've killed."

Crawley sobs while drooling, with snot coating his mouth and chin, mixing with the blood from his prior beating. When he doesn't answer her, Sam drills into his thigh, and the screams of agony bounce off the metal walls. The sound of bone and flesh being torn apart fills my ears in between his screams.

He finally starts talking, spilling names and details of all his atrocities over the years. Our men step closer, ready to tear him apart. How were we unaware of what he was doing? This is our city.

Once he's done talking and is a sobbing mess on the verge of passing out, Sam walks back to the table, laying the drill down.

She picks up the fillet knife again, studying it. When she turns, her eyes are void of any emotion. Like a predator approaching its prey, Sam walks back to us, stopping at Crawley's side. She lifts his shirt, revealing his pale sweat-slicked stomach. I know instantly what she's about to do, and I grin, stepping closer. Torture has always been more my area of expertise than Marco's.

With a single fluid motion, she slices him open. Crawley's intestines spill out onto his lap, the sight and smell overwhelming. I love to torture those who deserve it, but this is a level I've never seen a woman capable of. Then again, Sam is no ordinary woman. She's our queen.

Crawley's scream is soul-wrenching, piercing my ears. Sam steps back into me and I wrap my arms around her as we watch the life slowly fade from him. She leans forward enough to pull her Uncle Fred's gun from her back, and my eyes meet Marco's, seeing him stare at Sam with the same love and adoration I feel.

Sam pulls the trigger once it's aimed at Crawley's head. The shot rings out and his body jerks before going limp. Sam lowers her arm, and I pull her back tight against my chest as we stand here staring at his limp, lifeless body.

Sam seems to snap out of it, and she looks up at Marco, then tilts her head back against my chest, looking at me. I see the adrenaline fade from her and the turmoil in her eyes. I won't have that. She can't ever wonder what we think or feel for her. I'll always show her. I move quickly, scooping her into my arms, causing the gun to fall to the concrete. "You're a fucking queen," I say against her lips before kissing her.

Marco steps closer, fisting her hair, forcing her to look at him. I know she can see the pride and love in his eyes. "He's gone. Because of you, he can't hurt anyone again."

Sam nods, and her body melts in my arms as she trembles. Marco nods to the door, and I turn, carrying her out to the SUV. The only sound I hear is Marco barking orders for our men to kill the others and clean this shit up before he follows us out.

Marco jerks my door open when we return to the penthouse and takes Sam from me. I understand his need to care for her because it courses through my veins harder than the blood does. My only thought at this moment is getting her upstairs into the shower and removing all traces of Crawley's blood.

Exiting the elevator ahead of them, I open doors so Marco doesn't have to pause with our woman. Once in the bathroom, I start the shower while Marco places her on the vanity. He steps back, undressing while I strip Sam. She looks like a warrior with blood spatters on her, causing my dick to rise. This isn't the time. I chide myself while I remove her clothes.

Chapter 16

Marco

Once Sam is undressed, I take her hand, leading her into the shower. Steam rises all around us. The warm spray from both shower heads beats down on our bodies as Luca enters, shutting the door. I pull Sam close, watching Luca lather a washcloth to clean her. I run my fingers through Sam's long, silky hair, wetting it while Luca washes her.

My hands travel the length of her hair down the curve of her back. I trace every curve and dip of her spine down to her glorious, wide hips. I'm aching to be inside her, but this isn't the time. Sucking in a deep breath, I pull myself from my desire and get back to the task at hand.

My fingers work into her scalp, making sure I don't miss any strands before grabbing the shampoo. Sam tilts her head back into me, closing her eyes. A soft sigh escapes her lips as the water pelts her glorious, curvy body. I pour a generous amount onto her crown, then work it through her hair.

My movements are tender and calculated, so I relax her and remove all signs of the blood and grime from tonight. She is too precious to me to have anything from Crawley touching her.

The more I massage her scalp, the more tension leaves her body. We aren't just cleaning her. This is far more intimate. I want Sam to know she'll always be cared for and loved. Not just by our words, but by our actions.

The light floral fragrance of her shampoo mingles with the steam filling my nose as a low moan escapes her lips. I force myself to keep my movements slow and not reach down to stroke my throbbing length. Does she not realize what those sounds she makes do to me?

I stifle the groan threatening to escape before I reach up, adjusting the shower head closest to me, and rinse her hair thoroughly before letting Luca take over. While he rinses her body, I quickly wash and rinse myself. Once done,

I step out, grab towels, and dry her off. The three of us are all that exist in this moment.

We lead Sam to the bed, placing her in the center. Luca and I flank her sides, each of us holding her close. Sam's head rests on my chest while Luca holds her body, both of us needing to touch her. With my arm around her, I stroke her still-wet hair. Once she's settled and comfortable, I look over her head and lock eyes with Luca. We've talked about our future with her, but I can't wait any longer. With all that's happened recently, Sam needs a sense of family and stability. We'll be that and so much more.

He studies my face and I hope I'm conveying my thoughts. I can't wait another day to know if she'll agree to be our wife. I don't know how since we share her, but she needs to have our last name. Be not only the mother of our children but our wife. We'll figure out the details of how later. I want a ring on her finger. After several minutes Luca nods, hopefully understanding what I want to do.

I roll to my side as much as possible and reach into the nightstand. The velvet box I put there yesterday feels heavy in my hand. What will her answer be? Luca grins as I turn back with it in my hand. Good, we're on the same page. We both know this box well. Inside is our mother's engagement ring. An antique cushion-cut diamond with a rose gold band. It's a piece of our family history and a symbol of how much we love Sam. We vowed it would only be given to a worthy woman.

I pull my arm out from under Sam and open the box, revealing it to Sam. Tears shimmer in the light as her eyes widen. "Sam," I say, getting her attention. When her eyes meet mine, I continue. "I love you more than I can ever express. You're my everything. Will you be my wife?"

She nods, unable to speak, and I slide the ring from the box. Holding it between my fingers, I slide it onto her ring finger to the knuckle but stop there. I splay my hand on her stomach and she gives me a questioning look until Luca takes her hand.

He grips the ring with his fingertips and looks into her eyes. "Sam, you are the light to my darkness and the only woman besides my mother I've ever loved. Will you be my wife?"

LUST AND BLOOD

Sam chokes back a sob as tears spill down her cheeks. That beautiful smile tells me they're happy tears. "Yes. Yes to both of you," she says, looking between us. My heart's pounding in my chest at hearing those words.

Luca slides the ring fully onto her finger and leans in, kissing her. Once he pulls back, I grip her chin, tilting her head back, and dive down, unable to control myself. I push my tongue in, tasting every bit of her mouth. My future wife, my everything. I put all my passion and love for her into the kiss.

When she pulls back, the look on her face has my chest tightening. "It's impossible to marry both of you legally and I won't choose between you. I'll never choose." Before I can speak, her eyes go wide. "I have an idea. A crazy one, but it might take a couple of months to make it happen."

I smile down at her because, damn, this woman is everything. She's smart, fierce, loving, and vulnerable, all wrapped up in a perfect package. And I mean perfect. I wait for her to elaborate, but she grins mischievously at us.

"I need to look into something before saying more. Let's get some sleep. I'm exhausted." When she curls back up on my chest, taking a long look at her ring before settling, I know we won't be discussing this more tonight. I hold her close while Luca molds himself to her back, doing the same.

My mind is racing, trying to figure out what our little queen is up to, but I'm drawing a blank. I force myself to close my eyes and clear my mind. Maybe she'll tell us more tomorrow.

Chapter 17

Sam

The ride to the courthouse is a blur as nerves rack me. Today's the day. The day we've been working towards for 3 long months. I stare out the window while pulling on my suit jacket again. This is the most uncomfortable thing I've ever worn. My lawyer said it would look good if I dressed appropriately for the hearing. What does that even mean? Why are people so superficial, needing certain packaging to be taken seriously and heard?

"Stop fidgeting. You look beautiful." Marco's deep voice brings me out of my inner ramblings, and I look over and offer him a smile.

His eyes are on the road, but I don't miss the smirk. He and Luca took me shopping, hoping to get me in a dress if only for one day. When I chose a pantsuit, they were more than a little disappointed. "You two would think I looked good in a trash bag," I say with a raised brow.

Luca leans forward and growls lowly. "I'll always prefer you in nothing at all, mia regina." Damn these men, I think as I press my thighs together. Over the last few months, the pleasure they have shown me has been beyond my imagination. That's saying something because I'm pretty creative.

Once we arrive and park, Luca opens my door, helping me out of the SUV. I take a deep breath, inhaling the early morning air, still heavy with dew. Nothing has ever made me this nervous. Then again, I've never been inside a courthouse.

With Marco holding one hand and Luca the other, we walk up the large concrete steps to the double doors. When we enter, my first impression is that it feels more like a mausoleum than a place to start a future. I scan the vast area, seeing Mr. Kendrick, my lawyer, walking our way. He assured me just yesterday on the phone that it was more of a formality in my situation than anything, but that didn't settle my nerves. It feels like a stranger holds my plans in the palm of their hands.

MEL PATE

Mr. Kendrick approaches, shaking each of our hands, but I don't hear his words with my heart thundering in my ears. He leads us to an empty courtroom with all polished wood and cold marble floors. The air is thick with a musty scent and leather. Sunlight filters through three windows to my left, casting long rays of light across the room.

There's a quiet hum of voices from other rooms providing background noise. Marco and Luca each kiss my cheek following Mr. Kendrick's order to stay in the back of the courtroom unless the Judge asks them anything.

I follow his lead, sitting at a long table with two wooden chairs. As I sit calming myself, a bailiff enters, placing files on the bench for the judge. I fist my hands in my lap, knowing that the petition we filled out months ago is in that stack of files.

My eyes scan the huge wooden podium where the judge will sit. It's raised, putting them in a position to preside over the entire room. There's nothing fancy about it, but it still exudes authority.

Behind the bench, a door opens, and a woman comes out. She sits at a small desk to the side I hadn't noticed. When a woman in her mid-fifties with a stern face exits, I immediately know she's the judge by the black robe. "All rise," the bailiff calls out, and we stand.

I smooth down the front of my jacket and brace my palms on the table. All my focus is on the judge that will decide how I proceed with my plans. A stillness falls over the room as she sits and flips open a file. My eyes go to the nameplate on the bench. Judge Elena Harris. It suits her perfectly with the commanding presence she exudes. She isn't an imposing figure, but the way she carries herself says it all.

Judge Harris raises her head and sweeps the room before settling on me. "Miss Samantha Simms, the court clerk, will read the case details." My heart pounds, but I listen carefully as the woman from the small desk begins. Adjusting her wire-rimmed glasses, she clears her throat. "Case number 3479, Samantha Simms requesting a legal name change to Samantha Rizzo."

The judge's attention turns back to me and I meet her eyes. "Miss Samantha Simms under penalty of perjury. I'm going to ask you a few questions."

I square my shoulders before speaking. "Yes, of course, Judge Harris."

I see her lip twitch, but her eyes remain focused. "Are you seeking this name change to commit fraud or for any other unlawful reason?"

LUST AND BLOOD

"No, Judge, I'm not," I say loud and clear.

She leans forward, placing both arms on the bench and her face softens. "Samantha, please explain your reasons for this request."

I take a deep breath knowing she would ask me this, but my past is always painful to talk about. "Your Honor, my reasons are deeply personal. My family died in a house fire when I was very young with only myself and Uncle surviving. He died several months ago, leaving no other family ties. The name I carry holds pain and loss. I want to leave all that behind."

Her eyes hold understanding as she studies my face. "Is there anything else you would like to add?"

"Yes Judge," I suck in a breath before continuing. "I've found love, Your Honor. However, it's with two men, Marco and Luca Rizzo." I pause at the shock on her face. I glance to the back of the courtroom, seeing my men. My pillars of strength. "They've been my support and my family through many rough times, and I love them. Since marrying both is illegal. I choose to take their last name. Not only to unite us as a family, but for our future children carrying all our names."

Judge Harris arches an eyebrow slightly, sitting straighter. "Miss Simms, that is quite an unconventional reason. However, I understand your first. Are you sure this is what you want?"

I smile, knowing that there's no doubt. "Yes, your honor. More than anything." My voice is firm. Thankfully, she doesn't look down, seeing me dig my nails into my thighs to deal with my nerves.

For the first time, the judge leans back in her chair. Her face is one of contemplation, looking from me to the back of the courtroom. I slowly inhale and hold my breath, waiting for her to speak. "I need to understand this fully. Why this route? Why not just marry one of them?"

I place both palms back on the table, satisfied she's willing to listen. "Because I love them both equally. They love me. We're a unit and I won't ever choose. Changing my last name is the only way legally to acknowledge that."

Judge Harris studies me as if she's searching for something. She sighs, sitting forward. "Very well. Despite your unusual reason, I see no legal cause to deny your request."

Relief floods me, and I feel as though a weight has been lifted off my shoulders. I hear a mumbled, "Fuck yes," from the back and cringe. Can't those two hold their tongues long enough for us to get out of here?

Judge Harris slams the gavel down, quieting the room. "Samantha Simms, from this day forward, you will be known as Samantha Rizzo," she says, striking her gavel again. "I wish you all the best, Miss Rizzo. May you find the family and happiness you seek."

Miss Rizzo. She's the first person to call me that, and the smile that spreads across my face has my cheeks aching. Tears prick my eyes as I say a quick thank you. I turn, ignoring my lawyer, and walk straight to Marco and Luca, who are both grinning.

Luca picks me up once I'm within reach, swinging me around. "We did it," I say, laughing.

"Welcome to the family, Sam Rizzo," he says with a deep chuckle.

Marco stops us and pulls me from Luca. He threads his fingers into my hair and stares down at me with so much love. "Now we have a ceremony to plan. I won't be satisfied until everyone knows who you belong to."

Damn this man and his possessiveness. I love it and he knows it.

Once we thank our lawyer and get signed copies from the clerk's office, we leave the courthouse hand in hand. For all the pain in my past, my future now looks bright.

When we reach the parking lot, I see Jules and Lou waiting for us. As soon as Jules sees my smile, she knows the outcome. On our lawyer's advice, she didn't come with us. But seeing her here and ready to celebrate with us means everything. We embrace each other, laughing. Everyone that I love is right here with me.

The End.

Also by Mel Pate

Firehouse 77
The Hot Fire Chief: Firehouse 77 Book 2

Outcasts MC
Gia: Outcasts MC Book 1
Kane & Cowboy: Outcasts MC Book 2

Standalone
The Fireman Next Door: Firehouse 77 Book 1
Lust And Blood